Wings On A Guitar

August 16, 1977
If Elvis Hadn't Died!

Southern Charm Press

Printed and bound in the United States of America. All rights reserved. No part of this book may be reproduced or transmitted in any form or by any means, electronic or mechanical, including photocopying, recording, or by information storage and retrieval system—except by a reviewer who may quote brief passages in a review to be printed in a magazine or newspaper. For information, please contact Southern Charm Press, 150 Caldwell Drive, Hampton, Georgia 30228.

All photos of Elvis Presley used by Southern Charm Press and Glenda Ivey are copyrighted by Keith Alverson. Use of any of these photos without the expressed written consent of Keith Alverson is strictly prohibited
Contact info: Email: eponstage.net@charter.net
http://home.eznet.net/~bigtoast/KAlverson.htm

Copyright © 2002 by Glenda Ivey
All rights reserved.
Southern Charm Press, 150 Caldwell Drive, Hampton, GA 30228
Visit our Web site at www.southerncharmpress.com
The publisher offers discounts on this book when purchased in quantities. For more information, contact: toll free: 1-888-281-9393, fax: 770-946-5220, e-mail: info@southerncharmpress.com
Printed in the United States of America
First Printing: August 2002

Library of Congress Control Number
    LCCN: 2001087686
Ivey, Glenda
    Wings On A Guitar: August 16, 1977 - If Elvis Hadn't Died! / Glenda Ivey
    ISBN 0-9708537-6-9

Cover design by Book Cover Express

Wings On A Guitar

Glenda Ivey

Other books by this author
Silent Revenge
Ripped Apart

Scheduled for release 2003
Wings of Grace
(Sequel to Wings On A Guitar)

Dedication

I proudly dedicate this book to Elvis and the millions of fans who loved him for the kind and generous person that he was. He is greatly missed in body, but his spirit and beautiful voice, that he so lovingly flooded the world with . . . Will live forever.

Acknowledgments

My sincere thanks and appreciation to the following people who so willingly gave their time and inspiration to help with the completion and promotion of *Wings On A Guitar*.

Cliff Chandler, friend and fellow author, for suggesting the title for *Wings On A Guitar*.

Keith Alverson, for allowing me the use of the marvelous photograph of Elvis for the front cover and all advertising promotion.

Dr. James R. Biggerstaff, for providing me with medical information necessary for the accuracy of certain events in this book.

Kathy Williams, my friend and owner of Southern Charm Press, for her unlimited faith in my ability to write one of the few fiction books that have ever been written about Elvis Presley.

Suzie Housley, my Publicist, for her dedication and hard work in making *Wings On A Guitar* known worldwide.

Finally, wholehearted gratitude to my husband, Jake, and my many writer friends who have always given me support and encouragement. You are the inspiration that keeps me writing, and I love each and every one of you for it.

Author's Notes

Was Elvis treated with the wrong medications? Were they simply given to him in order to keep him in the state he needed to be in to perform long, grueling tours? Were downers given to him after a concert to bring him down from the natural high he felt when he was on stage? Were they given to him to help him relax enough to sleep? Or, were they simply used as a tool to get the most out of Elvis that could possibly be achieved to keep the money rolling in? Probably.

Were his doctors guilty of prescribing too many of these powerful drugs? Most definitely. How, and when did it begin and why was it allowed to continue for so long? Word has it that the doctors felt that if they didn't give Elvis the drugs, he would go to the street to get them, which could be dangerous. Is the real truth that they prescribed him large doses of drugs so he could keep on performing? Could be.

Then again, one must look at the reasoning behind the doctors involved who prescribed these powerful drugs in huge quantities. Was it merely because "*no* one said *no*" to Elvis Presley? That is a flimsy excuse. It's still difficult not to blame the doctors involved for prescribing Elvis so many of these drugs, because those doctors are they ones who have to take part of the blame for Elvis' addiction. However, there's another avenue to consider.

In the sixties and seventies, clinical depression was something doctors knew little about and certainly lacked the medical Information to treat a person with this imbalance correctly because of the absence of knowledge about this disorder. Now, years later, some of Elvis' family members suspect that clinical depression runs in their family. Since doctors at that time were basically unable to diagnose clinical depression, those stricken by it had to seek their own remedies. Without knowing it, Gladys might have suffered from clinical depression and her method for combating it was drinking.

While studying about the different types of depression from numerous sources, I've learned that many people suffer from manic depressive illness (bipolar disorder) which is distinguished by abnormal mood swings ranging from severe depression to exaggerated, undignified excitement. The usual pattern of bipolar disorder is one of increasing intensity and duration of symptoms that progress slowly over many years.

Bipolar disorder often occurs within families. Studies of identical twins raised apart found that about two-thirds of the pairs shared the disorder when one twin had it, especially if the twins were raised apart. Often, families of patients with bipolar disorder include members suffering from other psychiatric problems. Some studies suggest that a combination of bipolar and panic disorder may be inherited. It has long been observed that children of bipolar disorder parents often have a more severe form of the disorder than do their parents.

A manic occurrence usually comes on suddenly, often following a period of severe depression. Family members and friends notice that the person's mood is too "hyper" and that their behavior is strange. Some symptoms of a manic include rapid speech, disconnected thoughts, grandiose ideas and extreme irritability. Many people suffering from manic depression experience feelings of power, sometimes believing that they are godlike or have celebrity status, even as children. Some patients experience intense sexual energy.

In reviewing some of the symptoms of depression and bipolar disorder, which closely resemble those of clinical depression, people who knew Elvis well may recognize some of these symptoms having been illustrated by him.

1) Insomnia, or shallow, inefficient sleep patterns with frequent awakenings
2) Weight gain
3) Lacking the ability to concentrate or make decisions
4) Physical agitation or sluggish behavior
5) Feelings of guilt, helplessness and low self-esteem
6) Loss of interest or pleasure in life
7) Sad mood
8) Sudden outbursts of anger
9) Fatigue or loss of energy
10) Avoiding harmful situations
11) A strong dependence on rewards
12) Fear of being alone
13) Increased sexual activity

Foreword

Hundreds of books have been written about Elvis Presley since he died, and I've read most of them. Many were written by people who knew him well. They've written about the years spent with the greatest entertainer in the world. Many of these books are conflicting in fact; however, it was their story and they had the right to tell it.

Many were written by his family, as only they knew him. Then again, there were many family members who never knew the *real* Elvis. They knew how poor Gladys and Vernon had been when raising their son, and they also knew that Gladys was the backbone of the family. They remembered the sweet kid who worshiped, and worried constantly, about his mother. They knew that Elvis was giving to a fault, even when he was a child, and they were well aware that his talent was God-given. They also knew of some of his frustrations, his fears and his addiction to prescription drugs.

You're probably wondering, "Why another book about Elvis?" I've even asked myself the same question during the writing of this book. I believe the answer is a simple one. Like so many of those who appreciate his talent and the ability to share it, I don't want to let him go. I didn't in 1977, and I still don't. I enjoy the things Elvis and I had in common. I celebrate my birthday the same date he did,

January 8, his daddy and mine were both named Vernon, we both are of Cherokee heritage and my maiden name, Penney, and his last name both start with the letter "P."

I have tried to illustrate in this story how Elvis might have taken control of his life before it was too late. Many say that he was doomed and had reached the point of no return. I'm not sure I believe that. My belief is that if he'd been surrounded by those who *really* cared for him the way they portrayed, instead of trying to keep him alive for their own gains, that he might be alive today. You will find some language in the beginning of this book that is quite contrary to the way I normally write and may be offensive to some readers, but this is Elvis the way he was in those difficult days. I've made every effort to portray him as he was, and without that part of his personality brought into the story, it wouldn't be Elvis.

I am not one who was fortunate enough to have known Elvis Presley personally. In fact, when I grew out of my teenage years, I no longer cared for his Hound Dog and Blue Suede Shoes type music. Yet, when he began singing slow, melancholy love songs and recording Gospel music, I became his biggest fan. My home, and trips in my car, would be incomplete without Elvis' magnificent voice filling those spaces.

I own every song Elvis recorded and every concert that has been made available to the public for sale. I have tapes of all interviews that have been shown about him, as well as every movie he made. But do we see the real Elvis in those presentations? I don't think so. Elvis Presley was so much more than what we saw on the screen, or any of his live performances. He was a God-fearing man with the same desires and weaknesses of the common man. Elvis truly believed that his talent was given to him and that it was his responsibility to share it with the world, and he did, up until the day he died. The demands for him to exhibit his talent literally used him up in body, but certainly not in spirit. The magnificence of his voice will never leave this world, as he had to do.

With each new generation, young people who were not yet born when Elvis died, are beginning to appreciate his talent as much as those who followed him from concert to concert. My granddaughter loves listening to Elvis' music and she knows that when she's in the car with me, she will hear his voice. She also has a beautiful voice, and it thrills me to hear her sing along with him. I've told her about his life, his abuse of prescription drugs and his death. At her young age of nine, she is well aware that he gave of himself to the point of total destruction.

No one can sum up Elvis' final tribute to all of us better than she did last year. She stopped singing one afternoon long enough to say, "You know, Nana, I'll bet God is so happy to have Elvis up in Heaven singing just for Him."

CHAPTER ONE

September, 1978

"You're going to die, Elvis, if you don't start taking care of yourself. That's all there is to it," Dr. Brannon said without emotion.

Vernon, still pale and drawn from his recent heart attack, sat slightly slumped in a chair in the corner of the hospital room. "Listen to the doctor, Son. Please."

Vernon's intrusion into the conversation made little impact on Elvis. "I know how to take care of myself, Doc. In fact, I probably know as much as you do 'bout medicine."

Dr. Brannon knew he was dealing with a difficult patient, and in an effort to get through to this man, he was treading more carefully than he usually did with patients who obviously didn't want his help. "Perhaps, but we aren't talking about just medicine. We're talking about your whole lifestyle. I'm telling you, you're not going to be around much longer if you keep on the way you're going."

"I'm just tired — that's all. I need a rest. Been working too much."

"Elvis, I took care of only *one* of your problems last year. We managed to clean out your colon. My God, man, it was so impacted, it had turned to chalk. Your whole insides had slowed down and it was strictly because of the drug use. We removed a small portion of your colon because it was twisted. That's all we did."

"Yeah, I know, but you fixed me up. I don't have so many stomach problems anymore. I'm in good shape now, just gotta' slow down and lose a few pounds, I reckon." Elvis didn't want to be reminded of what had happened to him the year before. It had been too painful and embarrassing to the few who knew what had really happened. He was becoming irritated and tired of the doctor's persistence.

"And your being here now, what was that caused from?"

"I told you, I'm tired. That's all!"

"I'm sure you are, but you're taking too many drugs and they're going to kill you if you don't get a handle on it. You're taking this whole thing too lightly, Elvis. You were barely breathing when the ambulance got you here. You can call it anything you like, but the truth is that you overdosed on those pills."

"I got a lot of things wrong with me, Doc. That's why I have to take all my medication."

The doctor looked at Vernon, hoping he would step in again and say something, but he didn't. Vernon knew his son well, and he knew, regardless of the circumstances, that his boy would do exactly what he wanted to. He always had.

"You're not hearing me, Elvis," Dr. Brannon said with a slight irritation in his voice now. "Your blood tests showed a combination of powerful drugs that I haven't even seen in terminally ill cancer patients. I hate to say this to you because it's not pleasant for anyone to hear, but you're totally addicted to prescription drugs."

"Get outa' here — right now! Get outa' my goddam room! Daddy, call *my* doctor, I don't want this quack taking care of me! He don't understand."

Dr. Brannon closed the chart he'd been holding, and trying to hide his frustration, he said in a monotone voice, "It's your life, Elvis. I can't make you do anything, but I do know one thing for sure, if you don't get off of those drugs, the next time I see you, you'll be in the morgue."

"I *said* get outa' my room!"

Vernon was almost in tears because he knew the doctor was right. He couldn't bear the thought of losing his only son, but he couldn't do anything with him either.

"Did you hear him, Daddy? He talks like I'm some kind of street druggie. He don't even know me and he sure as hell don't know what I need!"

"Maybe you *have* been taking too much medicine, Son. The right amount is good, but you've been taking an awful lot of pills these past few years. Maybe he's right, maybe you do need to slow down on some of them."

Elvis was screaming now. "Slow down! Just tell me how I can do that? I have to work, even when I'm not able. Lots of people are depending on me, and I can't let 'em down. I can't stop working. I can't stop nothing. I gotta' take my medication to keep on going."

Vernon looked down toward the floor, as if he couldn't face Elvis. "The finances *are* getting pretty low, but it kills me to see you working sick."

"You know any other way to get money, Daddy?"

"No, Son. I don't." Then after a long hesitation, "You want me to call Dr. Carl?"

"Yeah, get him on the phone. Tell him to get my ass outa' this goddamn place. He should have already been here. He can take better care of me at home anyway. That quack, Brannon, ain't chopping on me no more! And they won't give me my medication here, and I need it!"

"Dr. Carl stopped in late yesterday afternoon, but you were sleeping."

Eager to change the conversation, and just as anxious to know if anyone knew what had happened to him, Elvis turned to his daddy. "Did it make the news?"

"Yeah, it did, but they just said you were in for rest due to exhaustion."

The all too familiar, slightly crooked smile that had lit up the spirits of millions for nearly twenty-five years, was obvious even through Elvis' bloated face. "Whew, I was worried 'bout that. Not as worried as I was last year though. Can you imagine what people would've thought if they'd known I fell off the toilet trying to take a shit! The press would have had a field day with that goddamn story. Is she gone, Daddy?"

"Yep, She moved out day before yesterday."

"Good. She was getting on my nerves anyway. All she wanted to do was dress up and go out. She has no idea what this world's even about. She don't even know what I'm about. I couldn't get through to her that my career puts a lot of stress on me and sometimes I just need to stay home and rest."

"Well, that's what happens when you keep picking the young ones, Sonny. All they wanna' do is have fun."

Elvis glared at Vernon for a moment before saying, "Are the guys outside?"

"Yeah, they're there."

"Are they worried about me?"

"Of course."

"Tell 'em to come on in, and get Dr. Carl on the phone."

A few of the guys almost stumbled over each other trying to get close to Elvis' bed and the others lagged behind as if they were reluctant to go in.

"Come on — come on in. I'm okay. Just got worn out's all."

"E, you scared the shit out of us."

His radiant smile once again lit up the room. "Aw, just got too tired and was sleeping so hard I couldn't wake up. Guess I took one of my medicines too close together. Don't see what all the ruckus is about anyway. And if you ever tell anybody, I swear, I'll use you for target practice."

One of the guys in the back put in, "Wadn't it a little more than that, E? I mean, you been in here for five days."

"And I shouldna' been. Dr. Carl shoulda' got me outa' here."

"He knew you needed the rest. We were all afraid it was your colon problem again. That was really a serious thing that happened to you last year."

Elvis laughed boisterously. "Guess that's why I'd had such a bad belly ache for so many years — too much crap inside me." Elvis very rarely smiled, but he laughed often when he wasn't depressed about something.

"Remember, the doctor said he didn't take all of it, didn't want to damage your colon. It's already stretched to the limit, so you gotta be careful from now on about what you eat."

"Yeah, he went over all that diet stuff with me again today. Said I have to eat lots of fiber and I don't know what all else. Anyway, I'm going home as soon as Daddy gets a hold of Dr. Carl."

"Don't know how you're even gonna get outa' here, E. You ought to see all those people outside. The hospital had to get the police to keep 'em from coming inside the hospital. We like to never even got outa' Graceland. I'll bet there are 300 people outside the gate. Hell, there's probably more than that."

Elvis was obviously pleased. He needed constant reassurance that people cared about him. The room was quiet for a moment. A few of the guy's eyes were red from having cried, and the others were obviously worried. Elvis had gained a lot of weight during the past year. He appeared to be bloated and his skin had a grayish cast. The appearance of white roots was evidence that his hair hadn't been dyed for a while. He looked gigantic lying in the bed. They all knew he had gotten huge, but seeing him lying almost flat, with his head nearly pushed into his chin from the heaviness gave off an appearance of doom.

"What?" Elvis asked. "Whatsa' matter with y'all? You look like I died or something."

One of the guys from the back finally spoke up. "We've been worried, boss. We still are. You don't look so good."

"You know me. I'll be all right — I always am. Just gotta lose some of this goddamn weight and get back to work. I'll be okay then. I guess the Colonel's in a wad 'cause this tour got canceled. I haven't heard from him, but he sent that huge bunch of flowers over there."

There had been talk that the Colonel was trying to sell Elvis' contract. He was getting tired of the cancellations and had decided that Elvis was about washed up. Vernon knew it and so did the guys, but they had kept the gossip away from Elvis, as they did all negative things. If it was true, he'd find out soon enough and none of them wanted to be around when Elvis found out. Through all their worry about their boss, the guys had almost enjoyed the past few days. It was a relief not having to hover over him constantly and watch every move he made, be available at his beck and call, and have the added responsibility of trying to keep him alive.

Elvis was in bad shape, they'd known it for a long time, but could do nothing about it. The boss wouldn't keep anyone around who criticized anything he did or said, especially about his taking pills to wake up, pills to stay awake, pills to go to sleep, then more pills to stay asleep. The new guys were also scared of losing their jobs. In essence, they were getting paid for doing nothing because Elvis had only performed three concerts during the past year. He'd had to cancel many and things weren't looking good for him at all. The guys didn't get paid much, but a few of them lived at Graceland and had no other expenses, Elvis saw to that.

They were all too aware of what had happened to the Memphis Mafia who had been with Elvis for so many years. Vernon had to let some of them go because the big money was no longer pouring in and some had quit because they couldn't take just hanging around waiting for Elvis to demand something from them. They were tired of it. It had been fun for them before, all the concert traveling, women in every town and the high living, but when that came to a near halt, life became boring for them. They couldn't go any place. Their job was to be right there at Graceland, or close by, just in case Elvis needed something. They were getting tired of babysitting and needed to do something constructive with their own lives. Besides, they were sure Elvis wouldn't be around much longer, and then what would they do?

The crowd that had gathered around the hospital hadn't diminished. They were desperate to know how their Elvis was. Twice a day, the doctor had gone out, made an announcement that Elvis was improving and suggested that they all please go home. His speech was to no avail. They wouldn't leave until the police came and thinned the crowd every couple of hours, then they were right back again. They wanted to be there when Elvis left the hospital and they wanted to see for themselves that he was all right.

There was no way to take Elvis from the hospital in any normal fashion. He was wheeled on a stretcher to the ambulance that had parked in the back at the delivery dock. As soon as his fans saw an ambulance pull from the side of the hospital, they began rushing to it in hopes Elvis was inside. As hard as the driver tried to get out onto the street before the crowd surrounded the ambulance, he couldn't make it. Short drapes were pulled on each side of the ambulance that prevented anyone from seeing in, but the fans screamed, "Elvis! Elvis! Oh, Elvis — Thank God you're okay!" They weren't certain it was him, but in case it was, they wanted him to know that they were there.

Getting through the gates of Graceland was even worse. Fans were huddled so close together in front of the gate, they resembled one blob of color. As far as the eye could see, down both sides of the street, people were waiting and praying. The ambulance driver turned his head slightly to the right and said, "I'm sorry, Mr. Presley, it's going to be slow moving getting through here."

"Don't worry about it," Elvis said. "They're my friends. They care about me, and I love 'em all. Don't be in a rush. Take as long as you need, just be careful and don't bump anybody."

Getting Elvis up the flight of stairs to his bedroom was even a harder task. He had ballooned to almost three-hundred pounds and the ambulance attendants took each step slowly and carefully, with Vernon following closely behind. "You're home now, Sonny. Doesn't it feel good to be home?"

"Sure does, Daddy. Hate those goddamn hospitals, and I ain't going back — ever again," he said with a half grin, but a determined look in his eyes, as if he genuinely meant what he'd said.

"I hope not," Vernon said softly, yet the tone of his voice let off the appearance of doubt.

Elvis was glad to be home again. Everything in the hospital was too white and too bright. He'd missed, more than anything, the dark solace of his own room and his own huge bed.

After getting Elvis into bed and propping three pillows behind him, Elvis thanked the attendants for their patience, when they felt like thanking him for the honor of being able to bring him home in better shape than they'd picked him up in the week before.

Vernon sat on the edge of Elvis' huge bed. "Want me to call downstairs and get you anything? Are you hungry?"

"I want my medication. They didn't give me enough in the hospital, and I know that's why I feel so bad."

"Don't you want me to wait 'til Dr. Carl gets here. He may want to change what's in your packets."

"No. I want my medication packets left exactly the way they are, and I want one now! You can't get no rest in a hospital, Daddy. They won't let you — always fiddlin' with you and takin' this test and that test. I need to get some sleep."

"Son . . . "

"What, Daddy?"

"Nothing . . . doesn't matter. I'll call down and have one sent up to you." Vernon wanted to talk to his boy about slowing down on those pills. He knew they were going to kill him eventually, but he also knew that subject was taboo with Elvis and that he would only get angry. He'd been through a lot and Vernon didn't want to upset him, but he didn't want him to die either. "Elvis, I need to tell you something before you take your medicine. You know how it affects you. One minute you're wide awake and the next minute you're out like a rock."

"That's 'cause I need to sleep," Elvis said defensively.

"I know, Son. But someone you haven't met before will be here in a little while, and if you fall asleep before he gets here, I don't want you waking up and finding a stranger in your room. Will you just wait a little while before taking your medicine. Maybe about 30 minutes or so?"

"A *stranger*? In *my* room?"

"Dr. Carl and I talked about it. You know you need someone here with you when you're sleeping. You don't need to be left alone."

"I'm not alone. I got four guys to watch after me."

"Well, you had more than that last year, and you almost died because none of them were around when you needed them. And the same thing happened again this time. I'm not taking that chance anymore and you shouldn't either."

"Daddy, I ain't havin' no damn stranger in my room with me." Then Elvis let go of one his famous crooked grins and said, "If she's young and pretty and hasn't got big feet, I might consider it."

"It's not a *she*, Elvis. It's a male nurse. It'll be his job to stay with you anytime you're sleeping or alone in your room."

Elvis shot straight up in the bed like a rocket. "You think you're gonna stick a goddamn faggot in here with me! Oh, no — that ain't gonna happen! Hell, no! Not now — not ever, and that's final!"

Vernon had seen that same look on Elvis' face, even when he was a little boy, and that look had always meant exactly what Elvis' had just said, "final!" Subject closed, and he didn't want to hear about it again.

A slight tap on the door helped break the tension between Vernon and Elvis that had erupted so suddenly. Vernon got up from the chair slowly, hoping it wasn't the new employee he'd hired. He knew Elvis would go into the wild fit of anger that he was already building up to.

An immediate change of expression took place on Elvis' face when he saw Dr. Carl.

"So, how are you feeling today, E?"

"I'd be fine if someone would give me my medication and if Daddy'd stop talking 'bout puttin' some queer in my room with me all the time. That's the damn craziest thing I ever heard of and it ain't gonna happen, so you tell him to give up that idea right now!"

"First, I want you to calm down," Dr. Carl said as he approached Elvis' bedside and placed his black bag on the floor. "It's wasn't Vernon's idea. It's mine and it is absolutely necessary that you have someone in here with you who's attention is one hundred percent dedicated to taking care of you and nothing else."

"My guys take care of me, they always have. Especially the others who'd been with me so long. They loved me and they took damn good care of me. It took this new group a few months to get broke in, but after Daddy told them what they had to do, they do it. I don't need nobody else. I don't *want* nobody else takin' care of me 'cept you and them." After finding out that Vernon had not been the one responsible for suggesting hiring someone Elvis didn't know, he was not as firm toward Dr. Carl as he had been to his daddy a short while ago. Never liking to admit that he was wrong about anything, Elvis seldom apologized verbally, but he did it in other ways. He turned to Vernon, "Daddy, you look tired. You go get some rest. Dr. Carl and I will work things out."

"Okay, Sonny, but you listen to him good 'cause he knows what he's talking about." Vernon left the room and Elvis said nothing, waiting to see what Dr. Carl had in store for him. He was more serious than usual, and Elvis knew he wasn't going to like whatever Dr. Carl had planned.

"Have you taken any of your medication since you've been home."

"No, and I need it. Daddy called down, but they didn't bring me my packet yet."

"Good. I want us to talk before you take any medicine."

"You don't understand, Doc. I need it. I'm shakin'. They didn't give me what I need in the hospital, and I'm feeling really bad."

"I imagine you are, but you can wait a few more minutes. I need to talk to you, and I need to make you understand just what condition you're in before you get all that medicine in you and fall asleep on me while I'm talking."

Elvis let out a groan. "Well talk fast 'cause my medication will be here any minute."

"No, Elvis. It won't. I've instructed the nurse not to send it up until after we've talked."

"What the hell's going on? Who do you think you are, anyway? Ain't nobody got the right to come into *my* house and tell me what 'they're gonna do' and what I *have* to do. I pay people to do exactly what I tell 'em to do, and the same goes for you!"

"No Elvis, it doesn't. You can fire me right now if you want to, but I'm going to tell you the truth about yourself *and* your condition."

Elvis said nothing for a moment, he sat glaring at Dr. Carl. His first impulse was to tell him to take his black bag, get the hell out of his room and never come back. Then he changed courses and decided to listen, and if he didn't like what he'd said, he'd fire him.

"Elvis, I am a simple doctor. I'm not a rich man and have no desire to be. I've only been with you for six months, and I've gone along with your desire for certain medications because I knew you were addicted to them, and I didn't want you going to doctors who don't care about you and will give you anything you want. But, I won't do that anymore. It's doing nothing but killing you, and I will not be responsible for that."

Elvis' anger was showing already. "They *do* care about me and they know I need my medication, that's why they make sure I have it."

"Well, I have to disagree with you on that point. The world is full of people who will give you anything you want, and do anything you want them to do, for a fancy new car and all the other expensive gifts you lavish on them."

"That's just 'cause I want to show my gratitude, and I sure didn't appreciate it when you sent back that Lincoln I gave you for Christmas. That showed me that you don't care about me."

"I'm sorry you took it that way, but I already have two cars, I don't need any more. Besides, there aren't enough expensive cars, or money, that will cause me to treat you in a way that I know will lead to your destruction. I just won't do it."

"What the hell are you saying!"

"I'm saying that the only way I will continue being your doctor is if you'll let me work with you and get you off some of these pills that you're addicted to."

"I'm not *addicted* to a goddamn thing! People who buy drugs off the street are addicts, not people who take prescribed drugs. I've never taken a pill in my life that didn't come from a doctor!"

"I believe that. Then again, unfortunately, some doctors will cater to a patient's wishes instead of what the patient needs, and I will not do that. Not for you or anyone else."

"And you really think I *need* you! Man, you're pitiful. This town's full of doctors who would jump at the chance to take care of me. And besides that, I can get anything I need from the doctors I know in California. They know how to take care of me. You're nothin' but a quack, just like that Brennan - always telling me what *I need!* Nobody knows what I need more'n I do."

"I agree with you on that point, Elvis. You've been taking so much of that junk for so long that you do need it now. I'm telling you, my friend, you won't be alive another year if you don't let me help you slow down on some of those pills. The combination you're taking will cause your whole body to slow down to the point that it will completely shut down and when that happens, there won't be any turning back. You'll die."

"You just tell me this, Doc. How in the hell can someone die from taking prescription medication? If the pills I'm taking are that goddamn dangerous, they would'n' be making 'em."

"Medication is designed for different illnesses and some are to be used for short periods of time, not for years like you've been doing, and certainly not the combination you're taking. Some medicine just doesn't react the right way with others."

"And you think I don't know that? I got my books, and I read 'bout medicine all the time. I know what I'm takin' and I know the side effects. The other pills take care of those."

"You've just answered the question yourself. You take pills with horrible side effects, then you take more pills to counteract those. That can work for a few weeks at a time, but after a while, that combination will start working on your body and completely destroy it. I'm telling you the truth, Elvis, you've about used up your days if you don't let go of some of them. Your previous doctor is being investigated right now for prescribing all those drugs to you. That should tell you something."

"Oh yeah, it tells me something all right, it tells me you're a quack just like Brennan! Get outa' here — get outa' my house! I don't ever wanna' see your shit-eating face again! And take your silly little bag with you, it probably ain't got nothin' but aspirin in it anyway!"

Elvis reached for the intercom by the side of the bed, pushed the button and said loudly, "Tell the guys to come up here, all of 'em and get my medication up here — right now!"

"Yessa, Mr. Elvis," he faintly heard before he released the button.

Elvis was hollering, "Come on in," before one of the guys even had time to knock on his door.

"Whatcha' need, Boss?" Ray asked at the same time he handed Elvis the small envelope filled with pills. Ray had been with Elvis for almost nine months, longer than any of the others. The other three looked nervous and Gary, the newest of the new crew, was shifting his feet from side to side.

"I need my medication first, then I want y'all to sit down 'cause I gotta' talk to you." Elvis opened the small white packet filled with pills, held it up to his mouth and dumped them all in his mouth at once, then washed them down with a huge gulp of water. "I wanna know who was in here with me last week when I couldn't get my breath?"

"I was, Elvis," Ray spoke up.

"I don't remember nothing 'cept having a hard time breathing for a long time. Next thing I knew I was in the hospital," Elvis said. "Did you see me having a hard time breathing?"

"Not really, E. You were okay when I left to go downstairs just for a few minutes."

"You mean you left me in here alone?" Elvis was calm, and that bothered all of the guys. Obviously Elvis was up to something unpleasant and it was unusual for him to be calm when he was bothered about anything."

"I was only gone for a few minutes. The guys were having a little dispute about some rules when they were playing pool and Gary called me down to set them straight."

"Didn't my daddy tell all of you when you first came to work here to never leave me alone when I'm sleeping? Didn't he tell you that I sleepwalk?"

All of the men nodded their heads, letting Elvis know that they had been drilled on that subject. "I was only away a few minutes," Ray said nervously.

"And in that few minutes I was up here, by myself, gasping for breath." Elvis said, still managing to keep control of his temper.

The room was hushed, no one said a word. Elvis waited for an answer, but none came.

"Tell me, Ray. What was I doing when you got back up here?"

"Well, I first thought you were asleep, then when I couldn't wake you up, I called an ambulance."

Elvis looked at each of the men, one by one, directly into their eyes for a long while, then said, "Okay. Y'all can go now. Tell my daddy to come up here." The four men walked out of the room slowly, knowing they should say something, but were not sure what to say. The door closed quietly behind them. Elvis shifted his heavy body around in the bed a little and looked toward the heavily draped window. He knew it was daylight outside and that plain, ordinary people were coming and going, doing regular things. Nothing about his life was plain or ordinary. It never had been. He thought about his dead twin and wondered what course his own life might have taken if Jessie hadn't died at birth. His thoughts traveled through the dirt-poor days in Tupelo and the way his classmates had made fun of him in high school. He thought about those times more often than people realized. He guessed that they would always be in his mind. He'd even found himself thinking of those hard times while he was on stage, looking out at the audience and wondering how many of those people had taken money they couldn't afford to spend just to come and hear him sing. He glanced at the clock. It was three-fifteen in the afternoon and he was getting drowsy.

Vernon opened the door slowly. "What's wrong, Sonny? You okay?"

"Yeah, Daddy. Just tired. Can you stay with me for a little while?"

"I'm here for as long as you want me to be, Son."

"I just talked to the guys. Ray said he was downstairs in the pool room when I was having such a hard time breathing that night."

Vernon sat silent and nodded his head, letting Elvis know that he either knew about it or wasn't surprised to hear.

"If he'd been with me the minute I started gasping for breath, I could have gotten to the hospital sooner, couldn't I?"

"Yes, you could have."

"And if Ray'd stayed downstairs longer and called the ambulance later than he did, I probably would have died?"

"That's what Dr. Brennan told you in the hospital."

"Daddy, they're not takin' good care of me, are they?"

"Nobody except your family will take the right kind of care of you, but the ones who are here all work in the daytime and that's when you're asleep. Why? Whatcha' got on your mind, Son?"

"I don't know - just trying to sort all this out. Do you really think I need that faggot staying with me?"

"Elvis, he ain't no faggot. He's a nice young man, about twenty-eight, I'd say. He's polite and a church going fella'. He'll know how to take good care of you 'cause he's a nurse, even if he is a man. And I'll tell you another thing, your momma would worry herself sick if she was alive, knowing your life depended on people who don't care for you as much as your family does."

A change of expression immediately cast itself on Elvis' bloated face. "I'd give anything in the world if Momma was here, she'd know what's best for me and tell me what to do."

Vernon looked sad, as he had many times since his son was a little boy. Elvis always depended on Gladys to give him advice and guide him the right way and that had always hurt Vernon. He'd felt like an outsider in the family, like there was no room for him in the closeness that Elvis and his momma shared. When Gladys died, Vernon was sure that Elvis would turn to him the way he had continually turned to his momma, but it didn't happen. "Dr. Brennan and Dr. Carl both told you what you need to do, Elvis, but you're paying 'em no mind."

"I heard what they said, but they're wrong. I know what I need, but at the same time I'm confused. You know that every room in this house is bugged 'cept mine and the rest of the family?"

"Of course, I know that."

"I used to listen to the other guys a lot. Most of the time they sounded like they were really concerned about me and loved me, then other times they'd make jokes about me. Now the new guys are beginning to do the same thing. I went through that in high school and it hurt a lot — people makin' fun of me. I thought it would stop when I got famous, but it hasn't. Seems like the only people who don't make fun of me nowadays are my family and my fans."

"They jus' don't understand you like your family does, Son."

"Nobody ever understood me but Momma."

Elvis' remarked cut right through Vernon's heart, as it had so many times before. He wanted to tell his son that he *did* understand him, but it wouldn't have done any good. "Well, what do you want me to do with that young fella' downstairs? Will you at least talk to him?"

"I still don't understand why in hell a man would want to do a woman's work." Elvis said, almost laughing.

"That doesn't matter. Only thing that does is that he knows something about doctoring, the same as a woman nurse does."

After some hesitation, Elvis said, "Well, tell him I'll talk to him, but I gotta' get some rest first. Tell 'em to stay here 'til I wake up."

"I'll go down and ask him, then I'll be right back."

When Vernon returned to stay with Elvis while he slept, he found his son already in a deep sleep.

CHAPTER TWO

Vernon didn't take his eyes off his son while he slept. Elvis' breathing was even and relaxed, but Vernon knew it wasn't normal sleep, it was a pill induced sleep. He had never seen Elvis look so bad. He'd lost a little weight after almost dying the year before, but within a few months, he had started gaining it back and now he was heavier than he'd ever been. Vernon worried about his son's heart. All the excess fat around it couldn't be good and since he'd had a heart attack himself, he was afraid that his son might be prone to the same.

His thoughts drifted back over the 27 years he and Gladys were married and the inconsolable state Elvis was in when she died. He remembered with shame the times he had been unkind to her and not tried hard enough to support his family. He wondered if Elvis held that against him. Often, during those hard times, Gladys was the sole supporter of the family. Back then, it didn't bother Vernon when Gladys had to wrap her swollen legs in bandages so she could keep working at the garment factory during her pregnancy, but it bothered him now. She should have been home resting instead of working until the very day the babies were born. Vernon wondered now, for the first time, if perhaps that was the reason they'd lost little Jessie Garon.

He remembered that day when they were living in Lauderdale Courts, the housing project in Memphis. Elvis was about twenty then and his singing career was just taking off. He'd stayed in his room for three days without coming out. When he finally did, he made one simple announcement. "Start packing, We're moving outa' this place!" On that day, Elvis took charge of their family and never let go of that control. But that didn't bother Vernon, it took the responsibility off his shoulders. From then on, Vernon lavished in the notoriety of being Elvis Presley's father, and he never again gave thought to having to work a regular job. His son had done for him what he couldn't do for his son.

And now, his own divorce plagued him. Had he made a mistake by marrying Dee? Was he looking for all the things Gladys was not? Was he looking for a woman to love him more than she loved her son, as Gladys had done? Did he want a fun filled life to replace the one he'd had with Elvis' mother who was always either sick or worried to death about Elvis? He'd engulfed her every waking moment from the day he was born until the day she died. There had always been little room for Vernon.

Elvis' slurred words interrupted Vernon's remembrances of the past. "What time is it, Daddy?"

"Almost seven."

"In the morning?"

"No, Son. It's evening time."

"I didn't sleep long."

"Not too long, but you don't look as tired as you did."

"Are my pills here?"

"You took them before you went to sleep, remember?"

"No, I mean the ones I take when I wake up?"

"I haven't called down for more. Why don't you try to get up and move around a little. Maybe you don't need to take anything right now?"

"I know what I need! And I know *when* I need it!"

"I'll get them for you," Vernon said, knowing that Elvis

would get mad if anything more was said about it.

"Tell Ray to bring 'em. I want him to help me get up, and I need my hair washed. Then I'll talk to that little faggot you got waiting downstairs, if he's still there."

"He's still waiting."

Ray tapped on the door, fearing the wrath that was sure to be waiting. He was surprised when Elvis acted as if nothing had happened earlier. He was friendly and seemed to have forgotten about the serious questioning he'd put Ray through before.

"Did you bring my medication?"

"Sure did."

After Elvis swallowed 10-12 pills in one gulp, he said, "Have you seen that little faggot they hired to babysit me?" Elvis asked, with a huge grin.

"I met him and he's not so little. He seems nice enough, but the guys and I are wondering what position that puts us in. You know, that's kinda' been our main job lately, taking care of you. Now if someone else is gonna do it, where does that put us?"

"Aw, that ain't nothin' to worry 'bout," Elvis said calmly. "I gotta hurry and get in shape for the next tour. Y'all will have plenty to do then. Besides, he won't be here but a few days anyway, if he's here at all. I gotta talk to him first. Don't want to wake up with the little sonofabitch in my bed, trying to mess with me. Then I'd have to kill him." Elvis wasn't grinning now. He was serious.

Ray had to call one of the other guys to help him get Elvis out of bed. Elvis couldn't help at all, he was like dead weight and had to be lifted.

"Man, I'm weaker than I thought," Elvis said, always in denial and making excuses. It wasn't weakness that prevented him from getting out of the bed by himself, it was his enormous body and the drugged-up state he was in.

Ray couldn't convince Elvis to get into the shower. His enormous body kept him from washing himself, and he wouldn't let *anyone* wash him. They had placed a seat in the shower stall, but Elvis was always afraid he would fall off, so he seldom took showers. While they helped him into clean pajamas and brushed his hair, one of the family members changed his sheets. That had to be done several times a day because he sweated profusely and that combination, along with not cleansing himself regularly, made it necessary to change the bed linens several times a day to keep the odor down in his bed.

Ray put several pillows at the headboard and they loaded Elvis onto the bed. "Anything else you need, Boss?"

"Naw, just send that 'whatever he is' up here so I can check him out." Elvis pushed his hair away from his face and wished he'd had his hair dyed before he'd gotten sick. It needed to be done weeks ago, but he hadn't felt like fooling with it and now his regular hairdresser was out of town. He hated for anyone, even his family, to see the gray shadow of hair around his face. And more than that, he hated looking at himself that way. A knock on his door brought the realization that he had to talk to this stranger and he wasn't looking forward to it. He knew the guy would not be there long anyway, so it seemed to be a waste of time for both of them.

Vernon walked in first. "Son, I'd like you to meet Wade Turner."

The six-four, blond haired young man didn't seem the least bit impressed by meeting the most famous entertainer in the world. "Nice to meet you, Mr. Presley."

My name's Elvis. My *daddy* is Mr. Presley." Elvis pointed to a plush, navy blue chair by the side of the bed. "Come and sit here so we can talk."

"Thank you, Sir."

As the burly, broad shouldered, young man came closer to Elvis, he realized that the guy was huge. *Then again, many queers are big*, he thought. There was a short silence, as if each man was waiting for the other to speak first.

Finally, Elvis did. "I'll be honest with you, boy. I don't

really know why you're here."

"It's my understanding, Mr. Presley, er ... Elvis, that I am being interviewed for the job of taking care of you."

"Are you really a nurse?" Elvis asked, trying hard to hold back a grin that refused to be held back.

"Yes, Sir. I am."

"But that's a woman's job, ain't it?"

"It used to be, but not so much anymore. More men are going into the field of nursing nowadays."

"Whatever in hell made you decide to be a *nurse* of all things." Elvis still wanted to laugh.

"Well, it wasn't my first decision. I really want to be a doctor, more than anything in the world, but the finances just aren't there. So, I'm doing the next best thing, helping take care of sick people."

Elvis was stunned by the boy's answer. Knowing well how it was not to have the money for something you wanted so desperately. Those days of feeling the same type disappointment would never leave him. He'd planned to ask the boy if he was a queer right away, but now that thought had completely left him. He even felt a twinge of guilt for thinking that.

"How old are you, boy?"

"Twenty-six, Sir."

"Don't call me *Sir* and don't call me *Mr. Presley*. I told you — my name is Elvis."

"It's kinda' hard for me to do that. My momma taught me to always address an older man as Sir."

A sweet smile of remembrance embraced Elvis' lips. "So did mine. And compared to you, I am definitely an older man, but I *want* you to call me Elvis."

"If you insist."

"I do. Now that we got that settled, what exactly are you plannin' to do for me?"

It was difficult for Wade to keep track of the conversation. He was stunned by the darkness of Elvis bedroom. He'd never seen anything like it. Everything in the room was royal blue with a touch of gold here and there. Even the walls were dark blue. Heavy dark drapes hung from the window facing the front of the house. Wade couldn't imagine why anyone would want to be holed up in such darkness during the daytime. "Well, Mr. Presley told me all about your health problems. It'll be my job to be with you any time you want me to be, especially when you're sleeping."

"But I thought you already had a job."

"I did, but Mr. Presley offered me more than I was making at the hospital."

"When did he do that?"

"Last week."

Elvis was furious that this had been kept from him. He came close to kicking this kid out of his house. How dare his daddy make definite plans without talking to him first? Elvis felt betrayed. "Did he hire you permanently?"

"Yes, he did."

"What if I don't want you here?"

"Then I guess I'll have to go job hunting."

"You quit your job to take care of the famous Elvis Presley, didn't you?"

"Not at all. I've already told you why I did it. Sure, you're a famous person, all right, but that's not the reason I'm here."

"Did my daddy offer you a lot of money?"

"Twenty-five more dollars a week than I was making."

"Hell, boy. You quit your job for a measly twenty-five more bucks?"

"Not only for that."

"Then what for?"

"Because your daddy said that you really needed help that you could depend on, and I'm sure I can do that."

"If you're here to try to get me to stop takin' my medication you can jus' walk out that goddamn door right this minute!"

Wade was uneasy, He wasn't used to that kind of language. "That's not what I'm here for at all. I was hired on to make sure that if anything happens to you when you're sleeping that you're taken care of right then. Mr. Presley said you've almost died twice because no one was with you."

"I guess that part's true." Elvis said. He liked this kid. He wasn't sure why, but he did. He especially liked the fact that Wade wasn't excited or intimidated around him. He treated Elvis as he would any other person and not the adored celebrity that he was. And he didn't appear to be afraid of Elvis either, like some of his guys had always been.

"Are you married, boy?" Elvis asked.

"No. Don't seem to have much time for women. I've been living with my momma and daddy to cut down on expenses and try to save money for medical school. When I'm not working, I'm usually studying medical books."

"It's a good thing you ain't married then."

"And why is that?"

"Cause, if you don't give women as much of you as they want, they'll leave your ass quicker'n you can take a pee. And you can take that to the bank because I know it's true. They all want the same thing when they get married. They want you there with them all the time. My career won't let me do that. Guess that's why I don't have much luck with long term relationships of any kind."

"I suppose it's the same for me. I wouldn't feel right getting married now because I don't have anything to offer a woman. Mostly I just work, study and go to church."

"Yeah, I know what you mean," Elvis said. "As for me, I mostly jus' work. Are you going to be living here at Graceland?"

"Yes, Sir. Mr. Presley said that's the only way I could have the job."

Elvis hesitated a moment before he spoke. "Well ... looks like you're going to be my new nurse-bodyguard." Then he let out a rambunctious laugh. "Guarding and nursing my body all at the same time, huh?"

"I'd like that opportunity, Mr. ...uh, Elvis. I just want to make sure you understand that I won't be here for a few hours on Wednesday nights or on Sunday mornings. I've already told Mr. Presley, and he said he'll make sure and be in the room with you the few hours I'm away."

"Where you gonna be?"

"Church, Sir."

"You go to church?"

"Every Wednesday night and every Sunday morning, unless I'm sick. I like to go on Sunday nights, too, but when I worked at the hospital, I had to work on Sunday nights."

"I think we can arrange for you to go to church on Sunday nights from now on if you want to," Elvis said matter-of-factly. What kind of church do you go to?"

"Assembly of God."

"Well — I'll be damned! I was raised in the Assembly of God church in Tupelo, Mississippi, just a block away from where we lived".

"You don't say?"

"Yep. Man, how I used to love to listen to those people sing. I'd get right up there with 'em when I was just a little fella' and sing loud as I could. Loved all the loud preaching and jumping and dancing around, too. Those people know how to worship the Lord."

"They sure do, and I felt empty inside when I had to work on Sunday nights and couldn't go."

Elvis knew that feeling well because it had been with him for many years now. He couldn't go to church, not to any church anywhere in the world. People would mob him.

"I sure wish I could go to church, just one more time." Elvis said in a solemn voice.

"You could, Sir. If you really wanted to."

Elvis didn't like his tone. "What do you mean, if I *really* wanted to! Don't you know who the fuck I am! I can't go *any* place anymore 'cept my concerts and then the whole goddamn police force is there, and I got people all around me the whole time I'm trying to get my ass on the stage. I can't even go to a goddamn movie during regular times. I have to rent the sonofabitch out at night when the fucking place is closed!"

Wade sat silent. He was uncomfortable and wondered how he was going to be able to keep quiet about the language Elvis used.

"What! You ain't got nothin' to say to that?" Elvis roared.

Again, Wade was silent. He was trying to think of something to say, yet all that he'd heard about Elvis Presley was that he had a horrible temper and Wade didn't want to be the cause of him being angry.

"You'll have to pardon me, Elvis. I'm just not used to all that cussing."

"Well, kid, if you'd lived the kind of life I have, and hung around the kind of people I've been around for more than 25 years, you'd cuss too!"

"I surely hope I wouldn't, Sir."

"Goddammit — I *told* you not to call me Sir!"

"I'll try to remember," Wade said without emotion.

Elvis was angered now and not caring what he said. His opinion of this male nurse was changing quickly, and he'd decided that this arrangement wasn't going to work at all. "I wasn't gonna ask you this, but *now* I am. Are you a damn faggot?"

Wade sat straight up in the chair. "No, I am not! Are you?"

Mimicking Wade, Elvis managed to pull himself away from the stack of pillows and sat straight up. He first let out that famous sideways grin, then broke into a fit of laughter that he hadn't experienced in years. Elvis held his hand out to Wade. "Welcome to Graceland, kid."

They both gave each other a strong handshake. There was a strange sort of communication in their eyes, an understanding of some type. An immediate closeness that neither one of them could have explained.

"Well, you might as well go on down and get yourself settled in. If you're hungry, just tell 'em in the kitchen what you want. They'll fix it for you. And tell my daddy I need to see him."

Wade was relieved knowing that Elvis had accepted him; however, he knew that he was probably facing the hardest challenge of his life. Elvis Presley needed so much more than constant watching. He needed to find a way to give back to the Lord what the Lord had given him. That was going to be the challenge.

As always, when Elvis beckoned for his daddy, he was there promptly. "Well, Sonny, what do you think about Wade?"

"He ain't no faggot, that's for sure, and I think I like him."

"I'm glad to hear that. He seems like a fine young fella to me."

"Daddy, did you know that he wants to be a doctor but he don't have money for medical school?"

"Now don't you start thinking 'bout paying his way through medical school, Elvis. The finances ain't that good right now."

"Wadn't thinking about that. I was just glad to find out he wants more outa' life than to be a man nurse."

"You need a good long rest, Son. You've about worked yourself to death and you're in bad shape. Now, before you jump on me, hear me out. You've been going non-stop since you were eighteen years old. Your body is giving out on you — plain and simple and you can't ignore that anymore. When you were younger, you could lose weight quickly, get a nice tan and be ready for a movie or a concert in less than a month. That ain't working anymore. You're forty-three years old, and if you don't listen to me, you're gonna end up dying young just like your momma did."

"I always bounce back, Daddy, you know I do."

"You won't this time if you don't start listening to people who care about you and get yourself well."

"And just where do you think our money is going to come from if I do all this slowing down you're talking about?"

"I been going over the finances, and it's true, they're in bad shape, but there's gotta be a way for you to take at least some time off and get yourself well."

"Have you lost your mind, Daddy? Too many people depend on me for a living. I can't take time off. I gotta get in shape for that tour next month."

"Son, you barely got through the last concert. The guys had to help you get on and off the stage. People are beginning to notice your weight and you don't need to be out there performing looking like you do. And it's gonna take a lot longer than a month for you to be like you should be up on that stage. Your career is gonna go straight downhill if you don't shape up and give your fans the kind of shows you've always given them."

"And what the hell's wrong with my shows!"

Vernon knew he was stepping on dangerous ground. He knew that Elvis' temper was as bad as his momma's had been, if not worse, but this time Vernon didn't care how mad Elvis got. His career and his life was at stake. "Your shows are different. You can hardly bend over anymore to kiss the girls, you've gotten where you just kinda' stand in one spot during the whole show and you're even forgetting words to songs you've been singing for twenty years or more. That's what's happening. I know you don't want to hear it, but you also know I'd never lie to you."

"My fans love me. They don't care if I'm a few pounds overweight, besides, I can lose this weight before concert time."

"You weigh almost three hundred pounds, did you know that?"

"Like hell, I do! I don't weigh no three hundred pounds!"

"Almost."

"What are the guys saying about this new guy being hired on to watch over me?" He was changing the subject. When Elvis didn't want to discuss something, or didn't want to be criticized, which few were brave enough to do, he always did one of two things, he either changed the subject abruptly or went into a rage of temper.

"Not much. But they're afraid of losing their jobs."

"They ain't gonna lose their jobs. I told Ray that. I need those guys for when I go on tour."

"Now's probably not a good time to be talking about this, but payroll has got to be cut. You've got so many people getting salaries and many of them ain't doing a darn thing 'cept playing pool, watching movies and just hanging around. We can't afford that."

"That's why I gotta' go on tour next month. And that's why I can't take a lotta' time off and rest! I got responsibilities!"

"No, Son. Not responsibilities. You're paying too many people you don't need to be paying."

"Like who?"

"Well, like having three pilots on the payroll, five guys who do nothing besides keep you company 'cause they sure aren't taking care of you like they were hired to do. You've got to stop spending so much money, too. You think nothing of buying another plane, or expensive car, buying houses for people, and I don't even know what all else."

Elvis' anger was beginning to build. He didn't like anyone telling him what to do with his money, not even his daddy. "So, what do you want me to do? Leave all our relatives without things they need? As long as I'm alive, I'll take care of my family."

"I'm not talking about family and you know it."

Elvis' voice was getting louder. "I don't mean to be disrespectful, Daddy, but here you are talkin' about me spending too much money and having too many people on the payroll and you go out and hire a damn nurse!"

"That's something that has to be. It's for your own good. You've taken care of so many people for so long, people that don't need taking care of. They've had a free ride off you long enough. It's time you start thinking about yourself and doing what's best for you for a change. I know you have fun buying all that stuff, but most of it's things you don't need. Nobody needs five airplanes and twelve cars. Nobody."

"Daddy, when I was growing up, we couldn't even buy the things we needed, now we can have everything we want. Don't that matter to you?"

"Of course, it does and your momma and I love you for everything you've done for us, but without you, Sonny, nothing would matter to me anyway. And I'm afraid I won't even outlive you if you don't take time off to get well. I've already buried one son, I don't wanna' live long enough to bury another one."

"Why in the hell does everybody think I'm gonna die! I'm sick and tired of hearing that shit!"

"Well, Son, that's what all the doctors said, and I believe them."

"Even Dr. Carl?"

"You know he did. He told you that this morning. He told me all about it."

"Awe, he didn't really mean it. He was only trying to scare me."

"No, he wasn't. He's serious. He explained it all to me. You're in real bad shape, Elvis. Your body's giving out on you. All the medication you've taken for so long has slowed your system down. That's why you have such a hard time going to the bathroom, your stomach's not working right. You eat all that food and it just stays inside you, gets clogged up in your colon and won't come out. That can't go on forever. They done took part of your colon out and what's left is weak. It won't take staying clogged up like that, and as long as you take all those pills, that's what's going to keep on happening."

Elvis laughed. "Daddy, are you trying to say that I'm full of shit? You already knew that," he said with a slight grin.

Vernon looked disgusted. He knew for a fact that if Gladys had said the same thing to Elvis that he would never have made a joke out of it. But he did with Vernon, and anyone else who tried to get him to change his ways. He either joked or went into a raging fit.

"Well, it's your decision to make," Vernon said sadly. "Looks like you won't listen to me."

"Don't worry, Daddy. I'm gonna be okay. I always am. How bad are the finances?"

"Pretty bad. If we don't pay that mortgage you put on Graceland last year, we're gonna lose it. They're calling the loan in 30 days."

"How much do they want?"

"With interest, the man at the bank said it's almost a million dollars."

"Awe, hell — we got that much in the checking account."

"No, Son, we don't."

"You mean we ain't even got a million dollars."

"That's what I said. You were only able to make three concerts last year. All the others had to be canceled 'cause you weren't able to do 'em. The expenses kept right on going all that time."

"Well, call them and tell 'em we'll pay it as soon as this next tour is over with."

"They won't wait that long. I already tried that."

"We ain't gonna lose Graceland, Daddy. This is momma's house."

"That's what I've been trying to tell you. You gotta' cut down. Stop spending and get some of these hangers-on off your payroll."

"That won't get us a million dollars in thirty days."

"I know that, but it's a start. I've tried to get another loan, and an extension, but with your income not stable anymore, they won't do it."

"Goddammit! I'm Elvis Presley! Of course, they'll do it!"

"No Elvis. Not this time."

"Then what are we gonna do, Daddy?"

"Best thing we can do is sell some of these things around here that you don't need."

"There ain't *nothin'* here that I don't need."

"You don't need five airplanes and twelve cars. We could get enough from some of those to pay off the mortgage."

"I can't sell my planes, I need 'em, and I don't wanna sell none of my cars."

"Then you figure out how we can get the money 'cause I can't worry about it anymore and can't do a thing anymore with you." Vernon was tired, physically and emotionally. He hadn't felt well since his last heart attack and the pressure was too much for him. He never could take pressure, even when he was well, but now it really put a strain on him.

"I'll figure out something, Daddy. Don't worry. You go on and get some rest. Tell Ray to bring me my pills."

Vernon looked at Elvis long and hard. He went close to the bed and put his hand on Elvis' swollen one. "No, Sonny. I won't. I'm not doing that anymore. I won't be the one responsible for getting you pills that are killing you. Don't ask me to do that again, because I won't."

"What!"

"You heard me. I said no, and I meant it. You gotta stop taking those pills."

"Get me my fucking pills right now — I need 'em!"

When Vernon walked out of the room and closed the door, he could still hear Elvis screaming. Vernon knew his son well enough to know that *no one* told Elvis Presley what to do, or what not to do.

CHAPTER THREE

Wade was in Elvis' room in less than five minutes with the packet of pills.

"You're a good man, Wade. You know I need my medication. Looks like me and you are gonna get along just fine."

Wade handed Elvis a fresh glass of water and watched again as this much beloved icon held the packet to his mouth and swallowed fourteen pills at once. He'd never seen anyone do that before. "Have you eaten anything since you've been home?" Wade asked.

"Not yet. Haven't been hungry. How 'bout you? Did they fix you something?"

"I had a sandwich."

"That's all? Man, there's *everything* down there. Why didn't you tell 'em to fix you a steak?"

"I don't eat heavy at night. The sandwich was enough, thank you."

"I need you to call Ray to come up here and help me up. I gotta pee."

"I don't need anyone's help. We can do it."

"I'm telling you, man, we need someone else. I'm so damn weak, I can't help much."

"Well," Wade said with a broad smile, "let's give it a try."

Before Elvis knew it, Wade had lifted him to an upright position, brought both legs to the edge of the bed and had him standing up. Wade held onto him during the short distance to the bathroom and held him up until he got through. "See, that wasn't so hard, was it?"

"Damn, man. You're one strong dude. My guys must be pussies. Always took two of 'em."

Elvis expected Wade to laugh like the other guys would have done, but he did not. He didn't like the way Elvis talked and wasn't going to pretend that he did. After getting him back into bed and comfortable, Wade sat in the chair next to the bed.

"So, what do we do now?" Elvis asked, "just sit here and look at each other?"

For the first time Wade laughed out loud. He had a pleasant laugh and Elvis was glad that he'd finally said something that amused his new companion. "That would be a waste of time now, wouldn't it?" Wade said.

"I'm normally up and about this time of night. I'm a night person. Don't like the daytime much anymore."

"Any special reason why you don't like the beautiful days God gives us?"

"It's not that I don't like them really. It's just that I've always worked at night and slept in the daytime. My body got used to it, I can't change that clock inside me now. Been doing it too long."

"I can understand that. Many people have night jobs and sleep in the daytime. I thought you just didn't like daytime."

"Hell, I don't know what I like or what I don't like anymore. I get so fucking bored when I'm not on the road."

"What do you do with your spare time?"

"Used to play a lot at night. Went to the movies, the amusement park and played football with the guys out in the yard. I got a racket ball court, too. But since I got so sick last year, I don't feel like doing those things anymore, so I jus' mostly read all night."

Wade was surprised to hear that a man with such bad grammar liked to read and wondered why reading hadn't helped his language skills.

"What do you like to read, Elvis?"

"All about different religions, why we're here and what we're supposed to do with our lives. Looking for all the answers, I guess."

"You didn't find the answers you needed when you went to church?"

"I was too young to question anything back then. You know, Wade, you said something before that's been bothering me. You said I could go to church if I *really* wanted to."

"Yes," Wade agreed. "I did say that."

"I can't figure you out, man. Surely you ain't so stupid that you think someone as famous as me can jus' walk in a church, like an ordinary man, and no one would pay any mind."

"In my church they wouldn't. We go there to worship God, not people."

"Are you saying that Elvis Presley could walk into your church, sit down in a pew like everybody else and not be paid any attention to."

"Well, they would be surprised, of course. But they would also be thrilled to see you there worshiping God, just like they are."

"You don't have to go to a church to worship God. I pray to him all the time, always have."

"I'm glad to hear that; however, the Bible does say that we're supposed to worship in the house of the Lord."

"You know, I am getting kinda' hungry now and my medication'll put me to sleep pretty soon. Guess I'd better eat something first. Call down and get me four double cheeseburgers sent up with lots of fried potatoes."

Wade couldn't believe it. He was sure that he had misunderstood. "Did you say *four* double cheeseburgers?"

"Whatsa' matter, you hard of hearing?"

"Not at all. That sure is a lot of food to eat at one time."

"I've always eaten a lot, 'cept when I was a kid. We was always so pore, sometimes supper was jus' cornbread and water. Now I can have anything I want to eat, and I want four double cheeseburgers!"

Wade had been warned that Elvis was difficult and could go into sudden rages when he was crossed in any way, but Wade stepped a tad further anyway. "How about me ordering you two burgers, then if you're still hungry, we'll get you two more."

"And what's wrong with me having all four when I want 'em?"

"It's not good for you. That's too much food for anyone to eat at one time. I'm not doing anything but trying to take care of you, Sir."

"I already told you not to call me *Sir*. Why can't you remember that? You either call me boss or Elvis."

"I'll call you Elvis."

"Then get my food up here to me."

"Two double cheeseburgers and a small order of fried potatoes — right?" Wade said with a half smile.

"Wrong! But you're gonna have to order me two more soon as those get here."

Wade let out a slight smile and said, "Okay, that's a deal."

Within fifteen minutes, Elvis' meal was delivered to his room. Wade put another pillow behind him so he could sit straight up to eat. Wade had been cautioned that sometimes Elvis fell asleep while eating, especially soon after he'd taken his medication, so he never took his eyes off Elvis while he took each bite and swallowed it. He'd never seen anyone eat so fast and take such big bites of food. *This man's an absolute glutton,* he thought.

Elvis finished off one burger in a few bites, then started on the other one. After two bites, he fell asleep holding the remainder of the burger in his hand. Wade knew Elvis didn't have that last bite still in his mouth because he'd seen him swallow it and had gotten him to take a drink of water right afterward. He also knew that Elvis would not sleep many hours. Elvis' doctor had told him that the pills weren't keeping him asleep as long as they used to. Elvis was becoming immune to the dosage and would soon be wanting something stronger.

Wade had brought his medical books to study while Elvis slept, but he couldn't concentrate. His mind was glued to this huge man sleeping within a few feet of him. A man who had the whole world at his feet, could afford anything he wanted and have any woman he wanted. He was someone who had control of everything, and everyone, except himself. Wade wanted desperately to help this man. Underneath all the fancy costumes and millions of dollars, he was still nothing more than one of God's children who had lost his way and didn't know how to get back to the things that really mattered in life. Peace and contentment. Wade prayed harder than he ever had that night. He asked for guidance in handling Elvis the right way so he would not anger him and be turned away. He needed to be there, and he needed God's help.

Glancing at the leftover food on the tray, and realizing that Elvis could wake at any moment and want more, Wade quickly took the tray, quietly opened the door and laid it on the floor outside. His timing was good. Elvis was awake a few minutes later.

"You still here?"

"Of course."

"You been staring at me the whole time I was asleep?"

"Not every second, but I'm keeping a close watch on you."

Elvis tried to shift around in his bed, but to no avail.

"Are you uncomfortable? Do you need to go to the bathroom?" Wade asked.

"My belly hurts. I always feel like I gotta' go to the bathroom, but when I get in there, I sit on the commode for hours and can't do a goddamn thing!"

"Have you always had trouble with your bowels?"

Elvis stopped and thought a moment. "For about ten years, I guess. It wasn't so bad back then though. I could take a laxative, or an enema, and it'd clean me right out. Now nothing seems to work. I know it's all the tension I'm always under. Tightens up the body a lot."

"I've been told about the medications you're taking, Elvis, and did some studying on them before I got here today. What you're taking is slowing down your digestive track."

"Then you find a way to fix it 'cause these doctors ain't doing such a good job at it."

"The only way to relieve that problem is to slow down on some of the pills you're taking. Maybe start eliminating just one a day and take it from there."

Again — someone is talking to Elvis about his medication. "I wish to hell everybody would stop telling me that. If my doctor didn't know I needed 'em, he would'n prescribe 'em for me. That's proof enough that I need 'em and can't do without 'em."

Wade knew he was once again stepping to the edge. "What good are the pills going to do when your whole digestive system shuts down completely and you can't go to the bathroom at all? Do you think you can live without ever going to the bathroom? And if they take any more of your colon out you'll have to wear one of those bags outside your body to catch the waste. That would be very unpleasant for you."

"Like hell, I would!" Here he was again, changing the subject. "I'm starving! What time is it?"

Wade stretched to look at the beside clock that was turned toward Elvis. "Quarter 'til five in the morning."

"Call downstairs. I want two steaks, biscuits and potatoes with gravy."

"I'd like for you to drink a couple of cups of bouillon first. It will give you nourishment and help kill your appetite a little."

"What the fuck is bouillon?"

"A liquid that tastes like beef, or chicken. You can have whichever flavor you want."

"You mean like soup with nothing in it?"

"Exactly."

"I'm hungry, man, no water that tastes like beef is gonna satisfy me."

"It may not, but it will be soothing on your stomach if you drink a few cups of that before you eat."

"You're a stubborn sonofabitch, you know that?" Elvis said, with enough irritation in his voice to show Wade that he was not happy with his suggestion.

"I've never thought of myself as stubborn," Wade said. "I do care about you and want you to be healthy again."

"How the hell can you care about me — you don't even know me. You're like all the others, you care about me because I'm Elvis Presley."

Wade raised his large, muscular body from the chair, took one step toward Elvis' bed and said, "You were right, Elvis, this arrangement may not work, after all. We have different goals. You're determined to let yourself die, and I'm determined *not* to let you die, not any time soon, that is." Those two things mix like oil and water and frankly, I don't want to spend all my time trying to convince you to do simple things that might help you feel better."

"You don't know nothin'! You ain't no doctor!"

"You're right, I am not a doctor, not yet anyway. But I do know how a person needs to eat to be healthy, and it looks like that's something you refuse to do. There are some things, regardless of how rich and famous a person is, they have to do themselves and it looks like you want everything done for you. If that's the case, there's nothing I can do for you."

"Hell, I thought you were jus' supposed to watch me sleep."

Wade let out a half sarcastic snicker. "That would be a mighty boring job for anyone, don't you think?"

"Not if they're paid to do it! Tell you what, you little

motherfucker, get the hell out of my house. I don't need you and I sure as hell don't need you telling me to drink goddamn colored water instead of eating. Go on — get outa' my sight!"

"I'm leaving right now, Elvis. But I want you to know something before I leave. I don't need to be exposed to a person who uses the Lord's name in vain and cusses the way you do!" On that note, Wade grabbed the two medical books he'd brought to the room and closed Elvis' bedroom door, not so quietly.

Vernon was upstairs in a flash. "Did you let that boy go, Elvis?"

"Sure as hell did. Still not convinced he ain't no goddamn queer!"

Vernon sat down and looked at his son for what seemed like an eternity to both of them.

Elvis' anger had reached the magnitude that came close to grabbing a gun and shooting another television, or throwing the nearest thing he could get his hands on across the room. "What? What the hell are you looking at me like that for?"

"Wade told me everything you two said to each other and what he'd tried to get you to do to help make your stomach feel better. You need that boy, Son. You're running out of people to care for you. I found you a nice church-going nurse to stay with you anytime you needed him, to help take care of you and to try to get you healthy and you treated him really bad. That ain't right. You've been treating everybody really ugly lately and people won't put up with being cussed at and insulted forever."

"Of course, they will. I'm Elvis Presley! They'll listen to whatever I feel like saying, do what I want 'em to do — *when* I want it done, or they're gone. Simple as that!"

"I don't know you anymore, Sonny. You've changed so much. You never used to be like this. You were always kind and nice to people, now you treat everybody around you like dirt."

"Well, thanks to those guys I trusted my life with for writing that goddamn book about me. I oughta' kill 'em for doing that to me."

"They didn't do it *to* you Elvis, they did it *for* you. They were trying to wake you up. Trying to let you know that you're living a life of self-destruction."

"You really believe that shit! They wrote that book 'cause they're pissed off about being fired and they wrote it to make money. The three of 'em put together don't have sense enough to write a book. They had to get that Steve 'somebody' to do it for 'em. Don't care what excuse they use, that's the bottom line. Money's the bottom line of every thing!"

"You're right about part of that. Money sure can make one's life easier, but on the other hand, it can make somebody's life sheer hell, too. Looks like that's what all your money has done to you and everbody who loves you."

"They're all out for what they can get outa' me — all of 'em. I don't remember nobody catering to me before I got rich, 'cept Momma."

"Does that include the family?"

"A few of 'em."

"Even me?"

"Yes, Daddy, it does. Not about the money, but it hurt me really bad when you and I was in the hospital at the same time, when you had your first heart attack. You told me I was the reason Momma died so young, cause I worried her to death and you blamed your heart attack on me. My momma would never say anything to hurt me the way that did."

Vernon felt a twinge of regret, "I should'na' said that, and I'm sorry I did."

"Too late to be sorry. You felt that way or you would'na said it. Jus' forget it."

"Well?" Vernon asked in a hurt tone. "What will you do now since you fired Wade?"

"Just like I've always done, let the guys take care of me."

"You mean the ones who nearly let you die."

"It don't matter no more, Daddy. I'd just as soon be with Momma. I'm so goddamn tired."

"You ain't gonna like what I'm about to say, but I'm gonna say it anyway. What makes you so sure you'll be with your momma? We both know she's in Heaven."

Elvis was stunned. He had never given any thought to *not* going to Heaven when he died. In fact, he'd wished many times during the past three years that he would die, just so he could be with his momma. He would never stop missing her, or needing her. "I'm not this bad son-of-a-bitch everybody thinks I am! I've done a lot of good things for a lot of people since I got rich, and you know it!"

"I know you have, but you've hurt a lot of people these last few years, too."

"God'll forgive me for that. He knows the kind of pressure I'm under."

"Could be," Vernon said, in a questioning tone.

"What! You think I'm gonna burn in hell like some murderer?"

"I don't know what I think, Sonny. Besides, I don't like talking about you dying."

"Death ain't so bad, Daddy. I've read up on it. There's the other side and it's a hellava' lot better'n this one."

"You're not thinking about taking your own life, are you, Sonny?"

"Hell, no! That's something the Lord *wouldn't* forgive me for. Besides, I got a lot to do still 'fore I check on outa' here." Elvis let out his famous sideways grin.

"So, what do we do now?" Vernon asked.

"Find a way to save Graceland."

"Then you gotta' sell something, Son."

"Let two of the planes go. Not the Lisa Marie, don't you *ever* sell the Lisa Marie! And keep the Jet Star, too. Will that bring enough?"

"It should, if I can find buyers quick enough."

"Then go do it and get my medicine up here ... and some food, too. I'm starving to death!"

As Vernon went down the back steps to the kitchen, he thought that his life was just about as messed up as Elvis' was. His own health was bad, he was having serious doubts about his girlfriend and wasn't sure he even wanted to get married again. His son was killing himself and there was nothing he could do about it. No one could control Elvis, except Gladys, and she was gone.

While upstairs in his dark room, isolated from the outside world, Elvis cried. Even the sound of his precious mother's name gave him a heartache that nothing could cure and Vernon had mentioned Gladys' name several times that day. Elvis missed her so much that his life had not been the same since she'd died. A hole, filled with loneliness, claimed a large portion of his heart.

He'd read so many books, trying to understand himself. He needed to know why *he* had been the one, out of so many other talented performers, to become so famous worldwide. He had always known that his talent was given to him by God, even though his momma and daddy both had beautiful voices, but he knew that lots of other people had beautiful voices also. Why had he been singled out to become so famous?

Elvis knew his career was in jeopardy, no one had to tell him that. He also knew that he needed to lose lots of weight. He'd seen some of the photos taken from his last concert. He didn't let anyone know that he was embarrassed by the way he looked, but he was. He hated the way he looked and his fans probably did too. Yet they still came in droves and still loved his voice, even though they were showing less excitement during his shows lately. He also knew that people were making fun of him and talking about him being on his death bed. Maybe some of the ones around him even wanted that. Elvis wasn't always drugged-out and in the incoherent state everyone thought he was. He was thinking and planning, just as he had done in high school.

Everyone thought he was shy and introverted back then, but he wasn't. He was thinking and planning, wanting to quit school and build a singing career, but he knew his momma would be heartbroken if he didn't finish high school. No one in his family had ever had a high school diploma, and Gladys was determined that he would be the first. And, only to make her happy, he was.

Wishing he could get out of the bed alone and down on his knees to pray, but knowing he couldn't, Elvis closed his eyes and began talking out loud. "Oh, Lord, please hear me. I need you so bad. I ain't got nobody else to talk to. I don't like myself, Lord. You made me the kind of person you wanted me to be, and I didn't pay attention. I remember when I was nice to everybody and I don't know what happened to me. I don't know why I get so mad and talk to people so bad, even people I love.

"Something's wrong with me, Lord, and I don't know how to fix it. I've asked you for so many things over the years and all you gave me that I asked for was my singing career. Why didn't you give me a little of what else I needed? I begged you not to let my momma die so I could have lots of years to make her life easy, but you let her die anyway. I begged you not to let my wife walk out on me, but you didn't stop her. I begged you to let me find my little brother's grave in that paupers cemetery, but you didn't help me. I'm not blaming you, Lord, I'm just wondering why you're not hearing me? I don't know what to do. I feel so alone, and I've never been alone since me and my brother were together in our momma's belly. Then, you even let him die.

"I know you don't always give us everything we ask for, 'cause sometimes it's not what we need, but I *needed* my brother and my momma and my wife. How come you didn't pay me no mind when I was talking to you? Looks like you ain't been listening to me for a long time, Lord."

"I got yo' suppah here, Missa Elvis," a sweet voice sounded from the hall.

"Thank you, honey. Come on in." Elvis didn't mind the interruption, he was through talking to the Lord anyway. It hadn't done much good in the past and he doubted that it would this time. "Is that big kid my daddy hired gone yet?"

"Don' know, Missa Elvis. I can ask yo' daddy?"

"Do that and if he's still here, tell daddy to send him up. And leave the door open. That kid knocks on it like he's gonna pound it down. He's got a fist like a gorilla."

"Yessa', I'll do that."

Elvis had just pushed his tray of food away from his stomach to the side of him when Wade walked in.

"What do you want, Mr. Presley?"

"Goddammit, I *told* you not to call me Mr. Presley! And sit down. I don't like you towering over me like some giant."

"I don't work for you anymore, Sir. I can speak any way I want to now."

Elvis grunted in irritation. *Damn, this little bastard's tough,* Elvis thought. "Well, you do now. I've decided that you might be able to do me some good, after all."

Wade sat silent for a moment. "I appreciate it, Mr. Presley, but I don't think so."

Elvis let the *Mr. Presley* go this time. "And why the hell not?"

"I came here to try to help you. It's obvious that you don't want my help. I've heard about how you have fired your employees one day, only to hire them back the next. I don't need that in my life. I don't want the worry of having a job one day and being kicked out the next."

"You've read that goddamn book those guys wrote about me, haven't you?"

"Yes, I did. Last night."

"And I guess you believe all that bull shit?"

"To be honest with you, I don't know what to believe. I wasn't around you then, so I can't say what's true and what isn't."

"Well, I can tell you! There ain't a fucking word of it true! And when I get better, I'm gonna sue the bastards, or

I may even kill 'em. They betrayed me with a pack of lies. They won't get by with it."

Wade didn't respond to Elvis' outlandish statement, yet he wasn't sure if it was far-fetched, or if Elvis really meant it.

"What do you have to say about that, boy?"

"Nothing much, That's between you and the Lord to work out."

"The Lord hasn't listened to me for a long time. No use in asking Him about this."

"Oh, He's been listening, all right. It's just that sometimes we want his immediate attention and 'we want what we want when we want it.' He doesn't act that way. He gives us what we *need*, not always what we *want*."

"Yeah, well, it ain't that way between Him and me. Used to be, but it ain't no more."

"And you're blaming Him for that?"

"Shit, I don't know who to blame. All I know is that He used to be there for me and He ain't no more."

"Maybe you're not there for *Him*."

"You know, kid. You gotta lotta' brass talking to me the way you do."

"I was raised to tell the truth, Mr. Presley. If it bothers you, then I'm sorry, but that part of me won't change, not even for someone as famous and rich as you."

"Hell, I couldn't trust you anyway. You can't remember a goddamn thing. You'd let me die sooner than the rest of 'em."

"And why do you say that?"

"Because you're so stupid you can't even remember *not* to call me Mr. Presley, and I don't even know how many times I've already told you."

"Oh, I could remember all right, but as I said before, I don't work for you anymore."

"But I told you that you can come back."

"That's right, you did. But you didn't *ask* me to."

Elvis shook his head. He'd never met anyone like Wade Butler. He didn't like his attitude, he didn't like the fact that he wasn't intimidated by him, but he did like him not being a wimp and agreeing with everything he said. He was growing tired of that from the others anyway.

"Okay, then. Will you come back to work for me?" Elvis said, in an almost defeated manner.

"Only if you'll listen to me and let me help you. If you're going to fight me about everything I suggest you do, then no, I will not."

"Damn, you got balls, boy! Elvis let out a huge grin. "Maybe that's why I like you."

"One thing you need to know before I start back to work for you."

"What else!"

"If you get mad and fire me again — I *will not* come back."

Elvis let out a roar of laughter. "Okay, you're the boss, but only until I get better. Now, I want you to call down and tell 'em to come get my supper and heat it up. Everything's cold now."

"Sure, I'll do that. Which do you like better, beef or chicken?"

"I like beef, but that's what I got here, two steaks. Damn man, I know you can't hear good, but I didn't know you were blind, too."

Wade acted as if didn't hear one word Elvis had said. He pushed the button on the intercom. "This is Wade. I'm in Elvis' room now and I'd like to know if you have any beef bouillon cubes? Good, will you please get the linens on Elvis' bed changed now, then wait ten minutes and prepare two large cups of beef bouillon, very hot, and send it to his room. Thank you."

"I told you, I ain't drinking none of that brown water."

Again, Wade pretended not to hear. He pulled the covers off of Elvis and brought his legs to the edge of the bed.

"How'd you know I had to pee?"

"I didn't," Wade said. "You're going to take a shower."

"No, hell no, I'm not! I'm scared to. I'll get in there and

bust my ass. Besides, I don't much like all that stuff about rubbing my body with soap every day like lots of people do. It ain't necessary."

"It is when someone's body smells as bad as yours does. Now come on, let's get you into the bathroom."

Wade sat Elvis down on the toilet and turned the shower water on.

"I ain't getting in there. I already told you that. I'm liable to fall and hurt myself."

"Yes, Elvis you are going to take a shower, and you will not fall. I'll get in there with you."

"I knew it all along! You're a goddamn faggot."

Wade just shook his head. He took his own clothes off, down to his shorts. "Let me know when you're ready to get in."

"Listen, boy. Ain't *no man* washing me. Never has and never will!"

Again, Wade tuned Elvis out completely. It was a battle of the wills and both were determined to win. "Can you take your pajama bottoms off, or do you need some help?"

"Hell, I'll fall off the goddamned toilet if I bend over. Done been that route," he grinned.

Wade walked over to Elvis and lifted him up. He pulled his pajama bottoms down and helped him get into the white padded chair in the middle of the shower.

"Whatever you don't want me to wash, tell me and I'll hand you the soap," Wade said.

"I don't want you washing none of me," Elvis said, with half a grin.

"What are you gonna do then. Just sit here and let the water run on you?" Then they both laughed.

Wade washed everything except Elvis private parts and Elvis made an attempt to do that himself. "Now hand me a towel quick, you done seen enough of me."

"I haven't seen anything I didn't see in the hospital every day. I don't care anything about your body other than it needs to be kept clean."

"All I ever worry about keeping clean is my hair."

"Obviously, and now that's clean too."

"I like having my hair washed in the sink better." Elvis said, sounding like a little boy.

"That's not a problem. We can do that from now on."

Tired from even getting up and being washed, Elvis willingly went back to bed. Wade picked up a cup of the steaming bouillon and handed it to Elvis.

"Damn, boy! Looks like somebody shit in this!"

Wade wanted to laugh, even though Elvis had used a curse word. It was the way Elvis said it, so seriously. "I promise you, Elvis. No one has. Now, please — drink it all, but slowly."

With a frown on his face, Elvis brought the cup to his mouth and took a small sip. Then he took another one. "Not as bad as I thought it'd be. Now, call downstairs and tell 'em to warm my supper up now. I'm ready to eat."

"I will, as soon as you finish both cups of bouillon." Wade sat down and watched.

"You remind me of some kind of peeping-tom, boy."

Wade laughed. "Guess you could call me your peeping-tom because I am watching you every moment. But I'd appreciate it if you don't call me *boy*."

"Well, you are. What's wrong with me calling you *boy*."

"Because I'm not a boy any longer. You want me to call you Elvis, and I want you to call me Wade. I don't much like nicknames."

"Well, excuse the hell out of me," Elvis grinned right before he took the last sip of the first cup of bouillon. That wasn't bad, but I ain't drinking that other one."

"Sure would hate for you to go to sleep without your supper." Wade said, sounding like a mother.

"I'm gonna have my supper!"

"Only if you drink the other cup of bouillon."

Elvis almost got mad, then thought, *What the hell. It ain't that bad. I'm just giving the kid a hard time — jus' playing with him.* He reached for the other cup and starting sipping, a little faster this time because this cup had cooled a little. "Are you satisfied now? I drank it all up, both of 'em, jus' like a good little boy. Can I have my supper now?"

"Certainly."

By the time the cook brought Elvis' meal to him, he was fast asleep, without taking any of his medication. Wade was sure he wouldn't sleep long. His body would be craving more drugs soon.

CHAPTER FOUR

Wade was tired. He'd been up all day, and it was three o'clock in the morning. He couldn't go to sleep, he had to watch Elvis. He had to make sure his breathing remained steady. *What have I gotten myself into?* he thought. *When will I sleep? I can't stay up twenty-four hours a day watching this man. Nobody could, and there's no one to relive me, at least, no one who could be trusted. Mr. Presley's not able and the rest of the staff have their day jobs here. I should have asked Mr. Presley about that.*

Wade had been told that Elvis stayed up all night, and he probably would again, as soon as he was able. Yet, in the meantime, Wade was stuck. He kept wanting to doze off and wished he had some coffee, but he was afraid that if he called down for some, he'd wake Elvis and he wouldn't dare leave him alone.

Just as he was about to doze off again, Elvis began making grumbling noises and tried to turn over. Without saying anything to him, Wade reached gently behind his back and helped him turn to the other side. Elvis made a strange noise, as if he was hurting. Wade waited a few minutes for it to subside, but it didn't. He had to wake Elvis. "Hey, man — are you all right?"

Elvis barely grunted. He wasn't awake yet. "Come on, Elvis. Wake up."

Opening his eyes very slowly, Elvis looked at Wade, but his eyes were glazed and he was still dazed. "What time is it?"

"Almost three-thirty in the morning."

"Oh, God! That was awful!" Elvis managed to say, sounding a little stronger now.

"What was awful? Are you in pain?"

"No — it was my momma and Jessie! Right here with me."

"Come on, let me help you sit up. You must have been dreaming."

"No, I wasn't. They were both here. Momma looked so pretty and little Jessie was a tiny baby in a crib, but he was talking to me like he was nine or ten years old. Didn't you see 'em? They were right over there." Elvis pointed to the corner of the room to the left of the door.

Wade knew for a fact that Elvis had been dreaming, but it would do no good to try to convince him otherwise, so Wade went along with him. "Did they say anything?"

"Yeah," Elvis said, rubbing his eyes, then running his thick fingers through his hair. "Jessie was calling me to come and be with him again. I told him I wanted to. I asked Momma if she was happy and at peace and she said no. She said she couldn't rest in peace until she knew I was okay and well again, like I used to be. I told her that I wanted to be with her and Jessie."

"And what did she to that?" Wade asked.

"She said I still got things to do here. Things to straighten out and make right again. I don't know what she's talking about. I always thought when you died and went to Heaven, you'd rest in peace for eternity. Now, Momma's telling me that ain't so."

"Do you dream a lot, Elvis?"

"Shit, man. I *never* dream. I did when I was a kid, but I haven't dreamed in years. And I told you, this wasn't a goddamned dream! They were here — right in this room with me. I told Momma I was gonna get up and give her and Jessie a big hug, but she told me to say in bed."

That must have been when Elvis was trying to turn over, Wade thought. "And then what happened?"

"I don't know, it got all hazy then. I asked her to come close to my bed so I could see her better. Told her I wanted to see those pretty little tootsies of hers and to give me a kiss, but she wouldn't come closer. She jus' kept fading away." By now, giant tears were streaming down Elvis' face. "Momma was everything to me," Elvis sobbed. "When she died, I wanted to die, too. I ain't been the same since she left me. They buried part of me when they buried her."

Wade took Elvis' hand and rubbed it softly. He felt sorry for this giant of a man, this international icon, a man worshiped and loved by people all over the world, yet he felt alone. "Do you think she'll come back, Elvis?"

Elvis was sobbing and wailing so hard, he could barely speak. "Don't know, didn't have time to ask her. She left me again, just like when she died."

Wade was convinced that in a short while, Elvis would be asking for his medication. He had already slept through one dose and would surely be needing another one, especially after this episode. "Can I get you anything? Maybe something to drink?"

"Jus' water."

He was beginning to calm down now and was more rational. "Wonder why Momma waited so long to come to me. I been asking her for years to come back, just so I could see her again. If she came back to let me know she was worried about me, why didn't she come years ago? I been messed up for a long time."

"There are some things we can't find answers for. You know that, Elvis." Wade said gently.

"Yeah, been looking for answers for a long time."

"I think your momma just gave you one."

"I don't know what she wants me to do."

"I think you do." Wade said, not sternly, yet not babying Elvis, which was obviously what he wanted.

"I don't know what I'm supposed to straighten out and make right, that's what she told me I had to do."

"She loved you very much, didn't she?"

"More'n anything in this world."

"Then it's *you* she wants to get straightened out. She wants you to make *yourself* right again and get off this crazy merry-go-round you've been on for so many years."

"This crazy merry-go-round you're talking about is my job, boy. It's what pays your salary."

"I know your singing career puts great demands on you; however, you could slow down your schedule, do half as much as you used to and still be a wealthy man."

"The Colonel won't let me slow down, and my fans don't want me to. I gotta' make my fans happy."

"So, you're going to work yourself into the grave to make your fans happy. I don't think that's what your momma would want. And as far as this Colonel is concerned, isn't he just another employee?"

"No, man. See, you don't know nothin'. The Colonel got hold of me when I was just a kid, jumping around on the stage, playing from one dingy place to another. I owe my whole career to him."

"Do you owe him your life as well?"

Elvis raised his voice slightly, but not in an angry tone. "You're a regular little smart ass, you know that?"

Wade let out a toothy smile, but said nothing. He'd found a way to get through to Elvis, at least for a while. His mother, that was the key. Only, he didn't know how long that would last. "No, I didn't know that. Is that what you think of me?"

"Naw, jus' kidding. I'm hungry, man. Gotta' have me some breakfast, and I ain't drinking none of that water that looks like somebody shit in it first, either."

Even through Elvis' harsh language, Wade couldn't help laughing. Elvis had a terrific sense of humor and his timing was flawless. Wade could understand why people wanted to be around him, even with his harsh language and demanding attitude.

"Just tell 'em I want my breakfast. They'll know what to send up."

Wade pushed the button on the intercom that went to the kitchen. "Elvis is ready for his breakfast now. Please bring him two eggs, the way he likes them cooked, three slices of lightly buttered toast, a bowl of fruit and two cups of chicken bouillon. And I'd like two cups of coffee for myself please."

"Hold it just a minute! That ain't enough for a fucking bird! They know what I want. Same as I always have for breakfast. Half a dozen eggs, cooked hard, a pound of burned bacon, fried potatoes and biscuits! Then I have peanut butter and banana sandwiches if I want 'em."

Wade paid no attention to Elvis. "Thank you," he told the cook.

"Who do you think you are, telling 'em what I'm gonna eat. They know what I like."

"Well, Elvis, I'm not ready for breakfast yet."

"I didn't say a goddamn thing about *your* breakfast."

"Oh, I'm sorry. I thought you wanted that amount of food for both of us."

"You're gonna be a pain in the ass, I can tell right now. Well, we have a problem, kid, 'cause I'm the biggest pain in the ass you'll ever run up against!"

"Could be." Wade said. "Now, let's get you up so we can get your face washed, your teeth brushed, clean pajamas on and I'm sure you need to go to the bathroom." Wade was trying to keep Elvis' mind occupied, minute by minute, hoping he could go a little longer before demanding his medication.

"My face ain't dirty, and I jus' put these jamas' on last night."

"I didn't say your face was dirty. It'll make you feel better — help you wake up. And you do need clean pajamas. You've had those on for hours, and you've been sweating like a pig. They're damp."

Wade proceeded into the same routine of lifting Elvis

up, bringing his legs to the edge of the bed and helping him to the bathroom. He had to hold onto Elvis while he washed his face and brushed his teeth. Wade didn't believe that Elvis was weak, he was sure the tremendous excess of fat on his slim frame couldn't accommodate all that heaviness and it was affecting his balance. Elvis had completely missed one of his packets of medication and hadn't even realized it. That, too, could account for the unstableness. Wade knew any minute the demand for a packet would come.

"After you finish your breakfast, I'll have your bed linens changed," Wade said, still trying to keep Elvis' mind away from his pills that were overdue, even if he had to keep him half-angry to do it.

"You little son-of-a-bitch, you're treating me like I got some kind of bad disease. Clean this and change that. Are you another Howard Hughes, or something? You scared of germs? You're gonna drive us both crazy with all this washing and changing clothes. You got some real hang-ups, you know that." Elvis was calm, but didn't appear to be kidding.

Wade grabbed a glass of water that was on Elvis' night stand and threw it violently across the room.

"What the hell's that all about!" Elvis screamed. "You got no right to throw nothing in my goddamn house! If any throwing's done — I do it! You hear that, boy?"

"Let me tell you something, Elvis. And we need to get this matter straightened out *right now*. I don't really mind you calling me boy, or kid, or any term like that. I don't especially like it, but you can get by with it. One thing you *can't* get by with is calling me a bastard or a son-of-a-bitch! Those two terms are direct slams against my mother, and that's one thing I don't take from anyone, not even the *great* Elvis Presley.

"And another thing, I'm getting sick and tired of you using the Lord's name in vain. Now I know exactly what your mother meant when she came into your room to let you know she isn't resting in peace.. You're cruel, Elvis. You don't take anyone's feelings into consideration but your own, and if you really were raised in the church, I'm sure your momma didn't raise you to talk like that to people, or order them around like they're slaves. Do you really think because you're so rich and famous that you have the right to treat people that way?"

Elvis looked at Wade hard and long. Wade didn't know what kind of fit of anger was coming his way, but he didn't care and he was prepared for it. "Aw, kid, I was just kidding. I talk like that all the time. Don't mean nothin' by it."

"It may not mean anything to you, but it does to me. It's hard enough for me to take listening to your filthy mouth, but you *will not* call me names that are an insult to my mother. And if you can't understand that, then you won't have to fire me again, because I'll quit!"

Elvis knew that Wade wasn't bluffing. The boy had balls, and even though Elvis was not keen on changing any of his ways, he admired the boy for that. He'd finally found someone who wouldn't cater to him and that alone, let him know that Wade was there strictly to take care of him and wanted nothing from him other than his salary. "What if I forget, and let it slip again?"

"Then I'm out of here, Elvis. For good."

"I thought you came here to help me and take care of me."

"That's exactly why I'm here. But I'm not here to have my mother insulted, or be ordered around like a trained dog."

Elvis laughed boisterously. "You're a mighty big dog, that's for sure. How much you weigh, boy?"

"Two hundred and ten."

"You don't look like you weigh that much."

"Guess it's because I'm so tall."

"I don't weigh much more'n that, and I sure do look a lot fatter than you."

Wade knew Elvis weighed a lot more than two hundred and ten pounds. He was soon finding out that Elvis was living in denial, about everything.

"Does that clock say five o'clock?" Elvis asked, looking surprised.

"Yep."

"At night"

"No, it's morning."

"Shit! What's happened? I don't eat breakfast 'til that time in the afternoon."

"Want me to call down and have them wait twelve more hours?" Wade asked, smiling.

"You little smart-ass." Elvis grinned. "Hey, I gotta have my pills. It's past time. I know it is."

"They'll do you more good if you'll take them on a full stomach instead of an empty one." Wade was still stalling, minute by minute.

"Who told you that horse-shit?"

"I learned it from studying my medical books," Wade lied.

"Than how come none of my doctors ever told me that?"

"I guess since you know so much about your medication, they thought you knew that too."

"You mean every time I take my packet of pills I gotta' eat a whole meal first? I'd look like a fucking elephant if I did that!"

Wade wanted to laugh, but didn't. "You don't have to, but they'd work better on you. You'd get more effect from them and quicker." Wade felt badly about lying because that was something he just didn't do. But he and Elvis were playing a game of the wills, it was just a matter of seeing who could win. Wade went into the bathroom, drew a glass of water from the faucet, picked up the packet of pills and handed them to Elvis.

Elvis looked stunned. "What the hell are you doing now? You told me I shouldn't take 'em before I eat."

"Aren't you used to doing what you want to do, when you want to do it?" Wade asked, stone-faced.

"You're not only a smart-ass, you don't know a shittin' thing about medicine."

Wade shifted in the heavily padded chair, rested his square chin on his hand and smiled, but said nothing. He was testing Elvis, trying to find out if this type of reverse psychology would work on him. Wade doubted that it would, Elvis was cunning and extremely intelligent.

"I know a little bit. Anyway, you said you wanted them, there they are." Wade said.

"I need 'em, man. I'm jumping inside. Won't be able to eat that bird meal you ordered for me if I don't take my pills first."

"Then take them. I'm not stopping you."

Elvis had never let anyone challenge him this way, and he wasn't sure why he was letting this kid do it. *Maybe I'm just too tired to fight it anymore,* he thought. "I'll take half of 'em now and the other half after I eat."

As soon as his meal was laid before him, Elvis let out a smirky grin. Man, this ain't no meal! This is not enough for a little kid. You're gonna starve me to death, that's what you're gonna do."

"Remember to drink your bouillon first," Wade reminded.

"At least this doesn't look like someone took a shit in it first." Elvis mocked.

"It's chicken bouillon."

"Oh, so chicken shit's not the same color as human shit?"

"Drink it, please, before it gets cold."

Elvis drank the first cup of bouillon without complaining so much this time. Then he reached for the other cup and downed that one also. He did eat every bit of his small meal and when he'd finished, Wade asked if he wanted him to call down and order his regular breakfast now.

"Naw, I'll get it in a little while," Elvis said.

"Then let's get you up, get your teeth brushed and your face washed. You need to go to the bathroom?"

"Jus' gotta pee. Damn, that colored water makes you pee a lot. And my face ain't dirty! You're gonna wear me out washing everything so much. You sure got a lot of hang-ups, boy. I don't see you washing your face every 10 minutes."

All the while Elvis was grumbling, Wade was helping him get on his feet. So far, there had been no mention of Elvis taking the rest of the pills he'd left in the packet. After going through the whole bathroom routine again, Elvis complaining a little here and there, Wade got him back into bed, praying all the while that Elvis wouldn't ask for the pills. He started talking quickly.

"How old were you when you first started singing, Elvis?"

"Do you have any fucking idea how many times I've been asked that question?" Elvis sounded a little annoyed.

"I'm sorry. I'm sure you've been flooded with questions like that. I was just curious."

"I started in church when I was a little boy. My momma said I'd leave her side and waddle up to where the choir was and just start bellowing out those songs."

Wade laughed. "I'd like to have seen that."

"I guess that's all I've ever really wanted to do is sing. Don't know why. Guess I was born with wanting that and nothing else."

"Did you think you'd ever become so famous."

"Never. I used to daydream about it all the time. In school, the other kids thought I was shy and withdrawn, but I wadn't. Just didn't have anything to say to 'em. They wouldn't have understood anyway."

"Understood what?"

"That singing was the only thing I wanted to do and it was the only way I thought I could make enough money to make life better for my momma and daddy. I was always thinking about that and how I could do it."

"You didn't want it for yourself?"

"Never did think about that. I wanted it for them so they'd never have to worry about a roof over their heads, or food on the table, like they did when I was growing up. We was pore, man. I mean *dirt* pore. Didn't have nothing much of our own."

"Well, you sure did accomplish that in a big way. But what about after they had everything they needed? Were you doing it for yourself then?"

Elvis looked away from Wade slightly, as if in deep thought. "Yeah, I guess so. Me and my fans. I owe everything to the Colonel and my fans. As long as they want me to sing, I'll keep on singing."

"I'm sure your fans must love you a lot." Wade knew he was asking silly questions, but he was trying to tire Elvis out before he asked for more of his medication.

"Of course, they do, and I love them."

"You know they wouldn't want to see you mistreating yourself the way you're doing, don't you?"

"Hell, they already know. Those bastards wrote that book about me. You said you read it. They broke the rules, man. Nobody says anything about what goes on in my private life, and that includes you. I still can't believe they did that to me. I loved those guys and thought they loved me."

"I read where they said they were trying to wake you up and make you realize what you were doing to yourself and others, as well."

"That's a crock of shit! They did it for the money. They don't care nothin' about me. I know that now."

"So, Elvis, what are your plans now?"

"I gotta get ready for that tour next month and you gotta help me. I know I look bad. Hey, you know anybody who could dye my hair for me. Can't stand this white showing. My hairdresser's out of town, and in a few more days I'll be all white-headed like my daddy."

Wade let out a little chuckle. "It looks great on him. He has beautiful hair, but you're right, it wouldn't quite go with your fancy jumpsuits. My next door neighbor is a beautician. I'm sure she would do it for you."

"Call her now." Elvis said, making clear that he was instructing and not asking.

"It's too early now. I'll call her when she gets to work. Maybe she can come late this afternoon after she gets off."

Elvis nodded a little, letting Wade know that was okay with him.

"Can't we open these dark drapes, Elvis? It's a beautiful day outside."

"No! Those drapes are never opened. I like it dark in here."

"Yeah, dark and ice cold." Wade said.

"I get hot easy. Don't like to be hot." Elvis' eyes were beginning to droop. Wade thought if he sat silent for a few minutes that Elvis might drift off to sleep for a little while before asking about his pills. Wade had to talk to Vernon about some kind of schedule. He couldn't stay awake twenty-four hours every day like he'd done this one. He was worn out himself, mostly from just sitting around, but he'd been up for one night and two days, and he was exhausted. He couldn't take the chance of falling asleep while Elvis was sleeping.

Wade waited a few minutes, waiting for Elvis to go into a sound sleep. He had to talk to Vernon. He very carefully pushed the button on the intercom and whispered, "Please ask Mr. Presley to come to Elvis' room and not to knock on the door. I'll be waiting for him just outside the door."

"Yessa," he heard on the other end.

Within five minutes Vernon was there with a frantic look on his face.

Wade had left the door open a couple of inches so he could look in on Elvis and listen for any unusual noises. "Don't worry, Mr. Presley. He's okay. He's sleeping again. It's just that we didn't talk about any kind of schedule for me watching Elvis. He needs to be watched constantly and I was awake all night long and am wearing thin now. I'm afraid I won't be able to stay awake much longer. I know you aren't feeling well, but will you stay with him just a few hours so I can get some sleep?"

"Sure, Wade. But I can't do much, don't ever know what to do with Elvis, and I don't have the strength to get him up if he needs to. I'd have to call one of the guys to help."

"No, sir. Please don't do that. Call *me* if anything unusual happens. I'll be right up."

Wade went downstairs to the room that had been assigned to him and collapsed on the bed. Being with Elvis during this short time had been an emotional drain, and he expected that it always would be.

Two hours later, the cook was pounding on his door. "Wake up, Missa Wade. Mr. Presley says something's happening with Missa Elvis! He needs you up there right now!"

Wade made a flying leap up the stairs. When he got in Elvis' room, he found Vernon white as a sheet, standing by the side of Elvis' bed, saying "Wake up, Son. Please — wake up!" Elvis was making weird noises and trying to toss around in the bed. His legs were jerking, his hands were shaking and he was sweating profusely.

"Shhh, Mr. Presley. Leave him alone. Don't wake him up."

"But look at him," Vernon cried. "He looks like he's having some kind of fit!"

"No, he's not. I believe Gladys is with him again."

"What!"

"When he was asleep the last time, he said that she was in the room with little Jessie, and they were both talking to him. I was sure he was dreaming, but it may be that she's really sending him messages that he needs. Please, let's let him be for a few minutes and see what happens."

"Are you sure you know what you're doing, Wade?"

"I believe I do. It's either that or he's craving his pills. He missed one whole packet and only took half of the last one. I promise you, I won't let it go for long. Why don't you go on downstairs and get yourself calmed down? I'll take care of him and if we need a doctor, I'll make sure he gets one."

Vernon reluctantly left the room. He didn't know what was going on. He had heard many times that spirits can come back from the other side and guide people, but he'd never known anyone it had happened to. He was scared.

Elvis was making unrecognizable sounds, as if he wanted to talk. Then he started humming *Rock of Ages*, missing parts here and there. Finally, he screamed, "No, Momma! You gotta tell me more! Don't go yet. I need to touch you — I want you to kiss me on the cheek like you used to." Elvis' own sobs woke him.

Wade took his hand and brushed Elvis' damp hair away from his face. "Your momma was here again, wasn't she, Elvis?"

Elvis couldn't talk. He could only cry. Wade wiped overflowing tears from Elvis' cheeks. "It's all right. Everything's okay now."

"No, it's not," Elvis said in a whisper. "I think she told me all she has to tell me. She won't be back again."

"Do you want to tell me about it?"

"I can't tell *nobody*. I want my medication."

Knowing that this was no time to try to stall, and that he probably did need some pills now, Wade gave them to him.

"This ain't all of 'em," Elvis said when he looked inside the small white packet."

"No, it's what was leftover from the last time you took them. Let's wait a few minutes. If you need more, I'll get them for you."

"Thanks, kid," Elvis said in a surrendering tone.

Wade wasn't sure if Elvis was still half asleep, or not in the mood to be demanding. He wished Elvis would tell him about his dream immediately, like he'd done before. *If he waits, he will probably forget, and I'll never know what upset him so,* Wade thought.

"Get my daddy up here. I gotta talk to him right now."

Wade did as he was told and then asked if he should leave when Vernon came in.

"Naw. You don't need to leave."

"Whatcha' need, Son?" Vernon asked, still shaken by the state Elvis had been in a short while ago.

"Did you sell that plane yet?"

"It's barely been a day, Elvis. I got word out to several people though."

"I want you to sell three of 'em. Keep the Lisa Marie and the Jet Star."

Wade could barely believe what he was hearing. *He's got five airplanes! What does any one person need with five airplanes?*

"And the cars, too. Sell 'em. Keep the Stutz, the white Lincoln and of course, Momma's car. We will never sell that."

"Are you sure, Son? Don't you want to think about it for a few days? We don't need that much money to get by."

"Do it, Daddy!" Elvis said, with more spark in his voice than he'd had earlier.

"Okay, if that's what you want."

"What are the guys doing?"

"Just hanging around to see if you need anything. Ray went out to get a haircut."

"When he gets back, get 'em all together, give 'em what you think's fair and tell 'em we can't keep 'em on the payroll no more."

Vernon gave Elvis a strange look that lasted a long time.

"I know what I'm doing, Daddy," Elvis said, sounding definite and very much in command.

"I didn't say you don't. But what are you going to do when you go back on tour? You can't go by yourself, and in the meantime, Wade can't stay awake twenty-four hours watching you. Who's gonna take care of you while he gets some sleep?"

"We'll find somebody." Elvis changed the subject abruptly. "Wade, did you call that friend of yours to come and dye my hair."

"Sure did. She'll be here around six-thirty."

"But she don't know what color dye to bring."

"I found several boxes of black hair color in your bathroom. If that's what you use, then she won't have to bring any."

"I guess my hairdresser left 'em in there."

Vernon sat silently, listening to the chit-chat between Elvis and Wade. Vernon was accustomed to Elvis' highs and lows and changing his mind from one minute to the next, but his son was acting out of character now. He didn't seem all drugged up, but Vernon couldn't understand why Elvis would want to sell some of his favorite things when it wasn't necessary. He decided not to do anything for a few days because he was sure Elvis would change his mind.

"One more thing before you leave, Daddy. Call the Colonel and tell him to cancel that tour next month."

Elvis had never canceled a tour that far ahead of time. It had always been at the last minute and because he wasn't physically able to perform. He'd never canceled for any other reason.

"Are you sure, Son? The Colonel won't like that one bit."

"Call him!"

CHAPTER FIVE

By nine o'clock that evening, Elvis' hair was jet black, he'd had a shower, eaten a light supper and had not asked for more medication. However, he hadn't cracked a smile, complained, or made one demand since he'd spoken with his daddy. Wade didn't know Elvis well at all yet, but he knew Elvis had something on his mind — something serious and important. Wade tried to change his somber mood by cracking a joke here and there, but Elvis only responded with a nod, or a slight hmm... sound.

"How do you feel, Elvis?" Wade finally asked.

"Tired."

"I know what you mean. We have to find someone to sit with you for a little while. I'm bushed. I can barely keep my eyes open."

"You go on downstairs and get some rest. I'll be okay."

"Oh, no. I'm not leaving you alone. You've had too many close calls already, and I won't be responsible for you having another one. Listen, I've got a buddy, a guy who goes to our church. He's a paramedic, but he lost his job last month when he brushed the side of the ambulance turning a corner and got the back end of this guy's Cadillac. The guy was a real stinker about it, so the hospital let him go. He hasn't been able to find a job yet and if he's home, he'll come over. How about me calling him to stay with you for a little while?"

"You mean tonight — right now?"

"If he's home, he'll do it."

Elvis just nodded in agreement. "But, you'll be close by if I need you, right?"

"I'll be here in a flash."

"What's his name?"

"Byron, but everyone calls him Buddy."

Elvis let out a "Ha!" Then said, "I don't blame 'em."

"Should I pass this by Mr. Presley before I call Buddy?"

"No, go ahead and call him."

Wade was off the phone in five minutes. Buddy could scarcely believe that he was actually going to be taking care of *the* Elvis Presley, even for one night. Buddy was thirty-four, a few years older than Wade, and a huge fan of Elvis' gospel music. He'd never been to one of his concerts, mainly because Elvis didn't sing many gospel songs in his concerts, and those were Buddy's favorites.

"He'll be here in about forty-five minutes," Wade said, in a much relieved tone.

"Then you need to call down to the gate to make sure Uncle Vester lets him in and then call Daddy and tell him."

"Will it be okay with Mr. Presley?"

"It's okay with me — that's all that matters right now."

Elvis sounded in control and completely rational, but Wade was uneasy about remarks he'd heard from Mr. Presley when he first spoke with him about coming to work there. Remarks about how Elvis would change his mind suddenly, for no apparent reason. And another thing, Elvis was being too agreeable, not testy like he'd been before he last dreamed of his mother. Wade wanted so much to know what Gladys had told Elvis in that dream, if anything.

Wade decided to tread on forbidden territory. "Elvis, you seem very relaxed, but sad. Are you sure you're okay?"

"Jus' got a lot on my mind's all. Gotta make a lot of changes. Daddy's been handling things all these years. His health is bad now and he don't need to be worrying anymore about me and all my affairs."

"Couldn't you hire someone else to take care of your finances?"

"Don't trust anybody but family to do that. My daddy ain't got much education, and many times don't do things right with the money, but at least he won't steal from me. I know that for a fact. Only thing about him that bothers me is that he watches every penny like it's the last one we're ever gonna have. And I know that's because he never wants us to be pore again."

"I understand." And Wade did. As much money as Elvis Presley made, he needed someone who would guard his money the right way. Books could be jumbled around in such a way, by an expert bookkeeper, that millions could be embezzled before anyone found out. "Buddy'll be here soon. Do you need to go to the bathroom before he gets here?"

"Naw, don't need anything 'cept something to drink. I want some ice water."

There was a small refrigerator in the sitting area in Elvis' huge bathroom filled with every type soft drink imaginable. Elvis didn't drink liquor, or beer, only sodas. Wade was still mystified by Elvis' demeanor. He was acting strange — much too calm.

Wade had left the door slightly ajar so Buddy wouldn't have to knock, in case Elvis fell asleep before he arrived. Buddy had managed to get there in exactly thirty minutes. The excitement of even being inside Graceland, much less taking care of Elvis Presley, was almost too much for him to comprehend. He wanted to hurry and get there to make sure it was really happening.

"Come on in, Buddy."

Byron Davis was a tall man, like Wade, but a lot smaller framed. He wasn't particularly good-looking, but he had an air of kindness about him and spoke softly. A crop of medium brown hair gave evidence that he normally wore it shorter and needed a haircut. Otherwise, he was clean-cut and nicely dressed. His nervousness showed when he went over to the bed to shake hands with Elvis. "I sure am pleased to meet you, Mr. Presley."

"Same here," Elvis said, turning abruptly toward Wade. "You'll have to teach him the rules, boy."

Buddy gave Wade an uncomfortable glance. "It's all right, Buddy. There are certain ways Elvis wants to be addressed. I'll fill you in," Wade said in a reassuring manner. By this time, Wade was having a hard time even standing up. He'd never felt so tired. "Okay, guys. I'm going to leave you with it. Now, Buddy. Don't leave him alone in this room for a second. If you need me, the intercom is by the bed." Wade motioned for Buddy to follow him out the door.

"Listen, Buddy. If he asked for his packet of pills, call me. If he starts trying to toss around in the bed and starts making strange noises, or talking in his sleep, call me. He sleepwalks, but hasn't since I've been here. Write down when he goes to sleep and when he wakes up. I need to know how long he's sleeping. If he wants a lot of food, call me. If his breathing seems uneasy, you know how to check that. Did you bring your things with you?"

"Yeah, I brought everything."

"Good. Okay, go on in there with him. He talked quite a bit last night and earlier today, but he's dreamed twice that his mother came to visit him and that's when he starts trying to move around in the bed and makes weird noises. I need to know immediately if he does that."

"You got it, Wade. Man, I can't believe I'm actually taking care of Elvis Presley. Never thought in a million years that I'd be doing this."

"Forget who he is. To us, he's a man in trouble — a man who's going to die if he isn't taken care of, and he's a man with deep emotional problems. That's all he is to us right now. Understand?"

"Yes, Wade, I do. Now, you go and get some rest. You know I'll call you if the least little thing happens."

Wade glanced at the clock on the night stand next to the bed in one of the guest rooms he'd been assigned to sleep in. It was much more pleasant than being in Elvis' room with all the dark drapes and dark furniture. It looked like a tomb. That word struck Wade like a bolt of thunder. Tomb! *Oh no, Elvis is going to try to kill himself. That's why he's been so quiet and calm since his last dream, the one he wouldn't tell me about. I've got to find out what his mother said to him, or didn't say. Elvis is going to give up! He wants to die!*

Jumping out of the bed without even putting his robe or slippers on, he flew up the back stairs from the kitchen. He didn't knock on the door for fear of waking Elvis. Instead, he opened it slowly, saw that Elvis was sleeping again and motioned for Buddy to come out into the hall.

"What? What's wrong?" Buddy asked, surprised by the look of shock on Wade's face.

"He's going to try to kill himself, Buddy. I just know it. His medicine is in the bathroom. Don't leave him in there alone — not for one second! And if you feel like you're going to doze off, get me on the intercom. It's number 8."

"I won't. I slept most of the afternoon, I'm okay. Go on now, I won't let him out of my sight."

Still uneasy, Wade went down the back stairs to his room and crawled back in bed. As tired as he was, now he *couldn't* sleep. *That's what he's got on his mind, I'm sure of it. But he can't, not with us watching him every minute.* Those words of horror echoed in Wade's mind over and over until sleep finally took over and washed them away.

Wade jumped when the alarm clock rang at seven o'clock. He took a quick shower, dressed and was in Elvis' room fifteen minutes later.

Elvis was sitting up in the bed, looking calm and rested.

"Did you have a good night, Elvis?"

"I think I did." Elvis turned to Buddy. "How long did I sleep?"

"The first time, you slept two hours and you woke up hungry."

"What did you eat, Elvis?"

"The cook made me a peanut butter and banana sandwich and a milkshake."

"Just one sandwich?"

Elvis looked a little perturbed, "Yes, Mother Nurse, just one."

Wade looked at Buddy for verification and Buddy nodded, indicating that Elvis was telling the truth.

"He stayed awake for a few hours, we talked a little, then he slept for another three hours," Buddy offered.

Wade wanted to ask if Elvis had demanded his medication, but he wouldn't dare in front of Elvis. Besides, Buddy had promised to call him if Elvis asked for his pills. *How could he have gone so many hours without them?* Buddy wondered. Then his question was answered.

"Wade, get me my medication. Man, I'm feeling really jumpy."

"Sure thing."

Checking the packets in the bathroom, he was comforted to know that they were all accounted for. There were only two left, then the nurse who lived in the back of Graceland would need to replenish his supply. Before Wade came, they had been issued to Elvis one packet at a time; however, the first day Wade had arrived, the nurse brought him five packets. Wade took one of the empty packets from the counter, checked the pills closely from a full packet and put half of them in the empty packet.

When he handed the packet to Elvis, he knew by the weight of it that it wasn't full. "I need all of 'em this time, and don't try to talk me out of it!"

"I won't," Wade said gently. "But remember what I said, they don't do you as much good on an empty stomach. You had a light supper and a sandwich during the night, that's not much food to be putting so much medicine in your stomach."

"I ain't hungry and I need 'em all!" Elvis was determined this time, and he wasn't going to be talked out of it.

Wade went to the bathroom for the other packet and watched with sorrow as Elvis swallowed them all in one gulp. Buddy's reaction was much the same as Wade's had been the first time he saw Elvis do that — a look of disbelief. Wade needed to talk to Elvis alone for a few minutes before the medicine took effect because he might fall asleep again soon. "Buddy," Wade said, "go on down to the kitchen. The cook will fix you some breakfast. Then you and I will get together before you leave."

"Are you sure they won't mind. I mean, they don't know who I am, do they?"

"The cook does. She knows you were here last night. She's a doll and will be glad to fix you anything you want."

Wade closed the door when Buddy left the room. "Elvis, can we talk a little bit?"

"Whatcha' wanna talk about?"

"I know I've only been with you two days, but you've been acting different since you had that second dream. Are you sure you don't want to talk about that with me? I'm a good listener."

"Naw, I don't wanna talk about it."

"It must have really shaken you up, Elvis. You're like a completely different man now. I haven't heard you say one curse word since then. In fact, you've talked very little."

"I got a lot of thinking to do and a lotta things to work out and ..."

Before Elvis could finish, the door flew open and a relatively short, over-weight man with a cigar hanging out of his mouth and a huge flowered shirt that hung down below his hips stormed in. "What's this about you wanting to cancel the tour, boy!"

Elvis looked uncomfortable, like a little boy who had been caught in a lie. "That's right, Sir. I can't do the next one."

"And why the hell not?"

"I'm really sick and I have to get my self in good shape again before I can go on another tour," Elvis said evenly and with a lot of respect.

"You've got a whole goddamned month to get in shape! You're not canceling this tour and that's final! Understand?"

"I'm sorry, Colonel. I have to."

"Lemme tell you something, boy. I caught the first plane out of California when Vernon called me last night. You can't cancel any more tours and that's all there is to it. You're ruining your career. Anybody can get in shape in a month. I've seen you do it in much less time than that."

"Have you ever seen me looking like this, Colonel?"

The Colonel took a long look at Elvis. "You're overweight, but you can lose that in a hurry. You've always been able to do it before and you're *going* to do it this time! Besides, you need the money. Your daddy told me so."

"Yes, Sir, I probably do, but I'm still not going on this tour. In fact, I don't know when I'm going to do another one."

"What! I've got five goddamned tours set up for you and you *will* do every one of them! Whatever you think is wrong with you, you're not taking money out of my pocket. You can end up in the poor house if you want to, but I won't be going there with you. You hear that!"

"Yes, Sir. I hear."

"Well, then, are we over this nonsense? Made a trip all the way out here for nothing." The man was extremely agitated and Wade couldn't understand why Elvis didn't stand up to him more forcefully, like he did with everyone else.

"Sorry about that, Colonel," Elvis said. "You coulda' called instead."

"I could have, but I didn't. I wanted to talk about this to you face to face."

"I hate to disappoint you, and I'm sorry for being the cause of you not making a lot of money this year, but I don't wanna schedule nothing definite right now." Elvis spoke slowly, as if he was scared to speak at all.

"I'll sue you, boy! We've got a contract! No — I'll do better than that, I'll drop you, that's what I'll do! You're too goddamn much trouble anyway and besides that, you're all washed up as an entertainer. You've passed your glory days and they won't ever come back. Las Vegas won't book you anymore, the movies don't want you and now you're back to singing in small auditoriums like you did twenty-five years ago."

Elvis hung his head for a moment, then looked the Colonel straight in the eyes. "We've been together for a long time, Colonel. You done a lot for me, and I'll always be grateful, but I reckon this is the way it's gonna have to be. I understand if you don't want me anymore."

Colonel Parker gave Elvis a mean-looking stare. "You're pitiful, boy. You know that? Look at you, piled up in that bed like a sack of blubber, talking out of your head. It's all those damn drugs you've taken so long. They've destroyed you. I knew this day was coming. You're a nothing now! You hear me — a washed-up nothing!"

Wade watched tears stream down and around Elvis' swollen cheeks.

Wade could not imagine anyone taking Elvis Presley down to the level the Colonel had. Elvis was like a little child, taking a whipping. "Wow, he's quite some character," Wade said.

"He's got a right to be mad," Elvis said, barely above a whisper. "I would'na been nothing without him. He took me when I was a kid, just getting started, and carried me all the way to a packed house at Madison Square Garden. He knows how to promote people. I only know how to sing. He's a smart man. I feel bad doing him like this."

"Is he really going to drop you, Elvis, or is he bluffing?"

"The Colonel don't bluff. He's straight-forward and means every word he says. He don't play games with people. He meant what he said."

"What will you do without a manager, or someone to arrange singing engagements for you when you're ready to go back to work?"

Elvis didn't answer. He pulled his lips close together and nodded in a fashion indicating that he had no idea.

Wade took a closer look around Elvis' room. It really was tomb-like. Royal blue walls, blue-black drapes with gold tassels, royal blue velvet bedspread, everything in the room was dark. "Mind if I open the drapes a little, Elvis. It's awfully dark in here."

"I like it dark. I got bad eyes and the light hurts 'em. I got glaucoma — guess from all those bright stage lights for so many years."

"Maybe it would help if you put sunglasses on."

"It'd still be dark, Elvis said," with a slight, forced smile.

"Perhaps, but not as dark as it is in here now."

"You don't like my bedroom, Wade?"

"I'm not criticizing it, Elvis. It's exquisite; however, light is good for the soul."

"How you figure that?"

Wade thought for a moment. "What's your favorite costume color to wear on stage?"

"I have 'em in all colors."

"I know, but which color is your favorite?"

"White, I guess. Why?"

"I was just going to ask you the same question. Why white?"

"Cause it makes me stand out more, I guess. I wear a lot of dark costumes, but they all got lots of jewels on 'em. Makes 'em flashy and that's what my fans like."

Wade wished he'd studied psychology. He needed to get *inside* Elvis That's the only way he would be able to help him. After reading the book, *Elvis What Happened*, written by some of Elvis' closest friends who had been with him a long time, Wade wondered if even *they* knew the *real* Elvis as they thought they had. He was a complicated man, no doubt about that, given to outbursts of the magnitude that would closely resemble madness, then switching almost immediately to a congenial, fun-loving and giving person. That type person, would indeed, be almost impossible to live with. Wade doubted that he would know what to do with Elvis if he returned to that same type person after he'd recovered from his second near-death episode in a period of only one year.

Wade finally broke out of his worrisome trance so he could keep Elvis talking. "You said your favorite color to wear on stage is white."

"Yeah, I guess. Sometimes I feel like I do better when I'm wearing white."

"Hmm ... that's unusual. Do you have any idea why you think you do better when you are wearing white on stage?"

"Naw, not really, seems people notice me more. I get a better response from 'em."

"Then there must be something to that. Colors make a big difference in the way we feel about things. Color has the ability to control one's attitude."

"Never heard that."

"It's true. For example, the color red excites people, even to the point of agitation sometimes. It isn't a relaxing color."

"I got some red costumes. Guess that's good, don't want my fans to relax." He let out a grin, rarely seen in the past few days.

Wade continued. "Then, we have light blue and green, the colors of water and they're supposed to have a soothing effect on people."

"Guess I better not wear blue no more, or green. I don't want my fans relaxed while I'm preforming. I want 'em to be excited, like I am when I'm up there."

Wade laughed. "But remember, red can work the other way. It can turn people off sometimes. Especially religious folks. It might remind them of the devil."

"I've already been accused of that, back when I first started performing. Man, I've been accused of corrupting young people just by singing and moving around a little. Had cops in the audience many times, just waitin' to arrest me if I got 'out of hand'. That's when they called me *Elvis the Pelvis*. Damn, how I hated that name! Made me feel like some kind of pervert or something."

Wade was taken back. Elvis had said "Damn." Wade just then realized that Elvis had not said one curse word since the second time he'd dreamed about his mother. He wished Elvis would tell him about that dream because it had made some kind of serious impact on him, but he wouldn't ask again. Elvis had already told him he didn't want to talk about it.

"What about white, what does that do to people." Elvis seemed interested in this topic.

"White is reverend, holy like. Some folks say that wearing white is a tribute to God, especially church-going people. Ever notice on Easter morning how many people dress up in white, even the men?"

"I told you I haven't been to church since I was a young boy. Can't go no more like regular people so I don't know what they wear." Elvis knew exactly what he was doing when he wore white and he knew what it signified. His fans worshiped him. He didn't want to be worshiped and he hated being called *The King*. Many times from the stage, he'd told people in the audience that there was only one King, and that was our Almighty God. But he knew that he was portraying a God-like appearance when he wore white on stage. That's what his fans reacted to the most and he would do anything to gain their attention and give them what they wanted. Everything Elvis did was for a purpose.

"Hey, man, what's all this talk about colors?" Elvis asked, with a little more energy than he'd had in his speech since two days before.

"I was just wondering why you'd choose to wear white a lot on the stage, yet enjoy such a dark, closed-up bedroom."

Elvis' dark, shadowed eyes cut toward Wade quickly. "It's my business how I want my bedroom. This is where I find the most peace in the world."

"Because it's dark?"

"Naw, because it's different from the other part of my life. I spend most days around thousands of people — people I don't even know. Oh, I love 'em 'cause they're my fans, but all those people trying to grab at me all the time, screaming and hollering and those horrible stage lights hurting my eyes all through a performance, wears on the soul and the body. When I come home, I have to come down off all that and this is my place to do it."

"I can understand that, Elvis." And he did.

"Will you get Daddy up here. I need to talk to him 'bout some things."

"Sure, and I'll have some lunch while you two talk."

"I don't want you to leave."

Wade felt uncomfortable, not knowing what Elvis wanted to talk to Vernon about. He wasn't part of the family and didn't understand why Elvis wanted him there. But he agreed to stay.

Vernon was obviously upset when he entered Elvis' room. He looked almost angry. "The Colonel is irate, Elvis. Says he's gonna' drop you. Is that true?"

"That's what he said, Daddy."

Vernon was speechless. He sat staring at Elvis for a good long while. "What in the world's wrong with you, Son? You can't do without the Colonel and you don't even seem bothered by it."

"I'm not, Daddy. It'll all be okay."

Vernon let out a disgusted grumble. "And who do you think's gonna' plan your tours and get everything promoted for you? That man has made you millions of dollars and you'll let him go 'just like that' without even seeming to care."

"He's made lots of millions for himself, too."

"Sure he has, and he's earned every bit of it. You know that. He's dedicated the past twenty-five years to you."

"And he's made more money than I have doing it, and you know that's true, Daddy."

"Since the day the two of you met, you've never gone against the Colonel. He always knew what was best for you."

"Momma didn't think so."

"Well, I did — right from the beginning. I knew he was a good business man and that he'd do right by you and he has. He made you famous, you couldn't have done that on your own."

"You're right 'bout that, Daddy, but I don't need him no more and he don't want me no more."

"And what makes you say he don't want you anymore?"

"I heard the guys talking, several times before I went to the hospital about how the Colonel was 'shopping around' for somebody to buy his contract 'cause he thought I was washed-up as a performer."

"Aw, Elvis, those boys don't know nothing that's going on about business."

"They musta' heard it somewhere, they didn't just make it up."

Wade listened to every word, even though he felt like an intruder. Everything he was hearing seemed to be proving his theory to be true. Elvis didn't want to live any longer. *And how does Elvis know what people are saying in other rooms in the house. You can't hear a thing outside his door. Oh my goodness, he's got this whole house bugged. He knows everything that's going on.*

"It's just gossip, that's all." Vernon said, but he'd heard it also and was afraid this day would come. However, he never expected Elvis to be so calm about it. Vernon wondered if Wade was sneaking Elvis some kind of drug he hadn't been taking before. His son was too calm about everything since he'd been home from the hospital, especially the past two days. That wasn't like him at all. A change was coming over him and it made Vernon uneasy. "Well, Son, do you have any idea how we're going to live, and keep Graceland, if you're not going to work any more?"

"I didn't say I wouldn't work anymore. I just said I ain't going on those tours the Colonel had set up for me."

"So what are we supposed to live on during this time you're going to do nothing?"

Wade was seeing a different side of Vernon now. A side completely dependent on his son for his own living. His concern had turned to money and where it was going to come from so his lifestyle wouldn't be changed in anyway.

Elvis didn't answer that last question his daddy had asked him. "You put out the word to sell those cars and planes, right?"

"Yeah, we got one bite. I think he's interested if he can get the bank loan."

"Good. Now, we need to give one of the pilots some advance pay and let him go. Keep Gardner, he's the best and the most dependable and see if you can hire Wallace for less as a standby pilot. Don't need three pilots for two planes. We gotta' get rid of everyone working here that ain't family, 'cept Julie and she's like family. Nobody can cook for me like she can."

Wade was very uncomfortable now. He was going to lose his job.

Vernon looked in Wade's direction, but couldn't face him. "Elvis, do you really mean *everybody*?"

"Yeah, everybody that ain't family, 'cept Julie and Wade. Hey Wade, do you think Buddy'd come to work here full time?"

Wade was stunned. Elvis was issuing orders so quickly, he wasn't sure he was taking it all in. "Uh — yes. Yes, I'm sure he would."

"Is he married?"

"Yes. He's married and has two small children, and he needs a job badly."

"Good. Call and tell him to start today. The two of you can take good care of me, and I trust you."

Vernon looked angry. "Anybody else you want me to get rid of, Elvis? You know we have several people working around Graceland who are good employees, but they're not family."

"I told you, Daddy. Nobody works at Graceland anymore

who ain't family, 'cept Julie, Wade and Buddy. About those other people, don't we have some family somewhere who needs a job. They ain't all rich like we are, you know?"

There was almost a sarcastic tone to Elvis' voice and Vernon didn't like it. "What's gotten into you, Son? You never minded having people around Graceland before who wasn't family. In fact, over the years, you've had people living here who were nothing more than friends, or hangers-on, if there was even a difference. People who made a salary and didn't do a darn thing but hang around waiting to get you something."

"It won't be like that no more, Daddy. Now, you get a hold of some of our family members and see which ones are having a hard time. Give 'em a job and a let 'em live here at Graceland. We got two house trailers in the back that are probably nicer'n what they're living in now."

"One of them will be empty when I let the man go who keeps Graceland's repairs up, but the other one's got Dr. Carl's nurse and her husband living in it." Vernon said.

"I don't need a nurse no more. I got one and Dr. Carl ain't gonna' give me no more medication 'cause he fired me, just like the Colonel did."

Vernon's eyes opened wide. "What are you gonna do about your medication, Sonny?"

Elvis turned to Wade. "You can find me a doctor, can't you? A good one?"

So much was happening so fast, Wade was even taken back. "Sure — I mean, I got to know some at the hospital."

"Then find me one. And I don't want no woman doctor neither. Women know about a lot of things, but doctoring ain't one of 'em." Elvis finally smiled. "And he'll have to agree to come here to me at Graceland when I'm not able to go to his office and that would have to be at night. Can't you see Elvis Presley walking into a doctor's office during his regular daytime working hours? What a riot that would be. Besides, they wouldn't need him anyway if I was there," Elvis said, half jokingly. Then he got serious. "Bet you didn't know I can heal by the 'laying on of hands'? Sure can, done it lots of times, but can't do it for myself."

Vernon cut in. "Elvis, you're not thinking with a clear head at all. You always have a doctor go with you on tour. A new doctor ain't gonna be able to up and leave his patients to go with you all over the place for weeks at a time."

"Daddy, I'm not being disrespectful to you, at least, I don't mean to. But I'd like you just to take care of what I asked you to and not worry 'bout the rest. Get those planes and cars sold, get some of our family in here, give 'em jobs and a better place to live and me and Wade will take care of the rest."

"Elvis, you can't take care of nothing, you never have been able to. Hate to say this to you, Son, but you've been spoiled rotten since you was a little kid. That's not your fault. It's mine and your momma's, but it ain't changed since you got grown up either. It's just gotten worse. To save my life, I can't figure out how you're gonna get by without having people cater to you all the time and be at your beck and call the very moment you want 'em to. It ain't your lifestyle to do any other way."

Elvis motioned for Vernon to get up and come sit on the side of the bed. "Daddy, you know that you don't have the education to be doing what you've been doing all these years, and I know it's been hard on you. Your health's not good now either and I worry 'bout you. You been worrying 'bout me all these years and I want it to stop. Right now. Life's gotten too hard for you and that's never what I wanted. You're gonna be able to take it easy now, like you need to."

Vernon was almost in tears. "But Sonny, you don't have the business sense to handle all your stuff by yourself. It takes a lot of people and a lot of coordinating to get one of your tours on the road. Who's gonna' do that for you now that the Colonel's gone?"

"Don't worry, Daddy. I ain't gonna' be needing so much taking care of from now on."

Again, Wade was enveloped with that horrible feeling. *He either thinks he's going to die soon and he's getting everything in order, or he has plans to commit suicide. Thank you Lord, for letting him want Buddy to work here. Between the two of us, Elvis won't have the opportunity to do that to himself.*

CHAPTER SIX

October at Graceland passed with the usual burst of autumn shades, creating a spectacular display of color that surrounded the mansion like a protective, multicolored blanket. Elvis was gaining his strength back, but slowly. He had remained in the same somber state of mind he'd been in since he had last dreamed of his mother and made the radical decision of replacing most of the employees at Graceland with family members.

Elvis' colossal mansion was no longer alive with multitudes of people swarming about. The new family members who had been brought in to replace some of the previous employees were grateful, but at the same time, in awe of the status Elvis had gained since those poverty days in Tupelo. Some were distant relatives who had not been exposed to Elvis' climb to fame and had never been to Graceland before. They pretty much stayed to themselves, except when Elvis insisted they come to the house for family meals, which he did often.

Buddy was still in awe of Elvis, but not to the point that he didn't watch him every moment he was on duty. He still couldn't believe that he was working for Elvis Presley at Graceland and neither could his friends. They were always asking to come to Graceland to visit, but visitors were no longer allowed at Graceland.

Elvis spent a lot of time talking to his relatives, mostly Minnie Mae, his grandmother, whom Elvis had always called Dodger. No one could remember when, or why, Elvis started calling her that. He was hungry to know about his mother and daddy when they were young and spent hours listening to stories about his family before he was born. He was like a sponge, wanting to know everything there was to know about his relatives. He was surprised when one of his uncles said that he didn't know for sure if all the members of their family were really deeply religious, or if they went to church all the time because it didn't cost any money.

Thanksgiving was pleasant and plentiful. Wade and Buddy, whose wife and children had been invited, were the only ones there who weren't family members. Christmas was Elvis' favorite holiday, but he enjoyed Thanksgiving immensely because it *was* so close to Christmas. He was more jovial than he'd been in months. He'd lost thirty pounds, no longer complained about the small meals Wade ordered for him and had even taken Wade's advice to get out on the grounds and walk around. Because fans were always at the gates of Graceland, they stayed close to the house and most of the time they walked in the backyard.

Wade had convinced Dr. Lee Hunter, who attended the Assembly of God Church, to take Elvis on as a patient. Dr. Lee, as everyone called him, was in his late sixties and loved by everyone who knew him. He was kind, soft-spoken and had a genuine concern for his patients, even those who couldn't afford to pay him. When Elvis offered to pay Dr. Lee double the amount for an office visit if he would come to Graceland to see him, Dr. Lee refused. "My charge is my charge," he'd said. "No matter where is it."

Dr. Lee was well aware of Elvis' drug problems. He had called Dr. Carl and spoken with Vernon and Wade. He knew what he was taking on and felt comfortable with it. During the two months Wade had been with Elvis, he had been able to talk Elvis out of taking whole packets of his medication at one time, but that's the most he could do. Elvis needed professional help and Wade wasn't sure that was even enough.

On one of Dr. Lee's visits, Wade stayed in the room and watched as he and Elvis went through Elvis' medication and compared it with the book Elvis had about pills and what illnesses they were used for. Dr. Lee was able to convince Elvis that some of the pills, even though they had different names, shapes and colors, served the same purpose. Elvis was extremely knowledgeable about the medication he had taken for so many years, but he and Dr. Lee had bonded almost immediately and Elvis paid attention to him.

During the course of the next two weeks, Dr. Lee had changed some of the medication, eliminated a few pills and as a result Elvis was putting half the amount of junk into his body. It wasn't all easy, though. He went through a lot of unpleasant and painful experiences during that withdrawal time, and Dr. Lee, with his loving manner was by Elvis' side as often as he could be during those hard times.

Contrary to the type person Wade had heard that he was, Elvis complained little. He suffered the battle and had won half of it. Dr. Lee regulated the dispensing of Elvis' medicine in such a way that he was sleeping more at night and awake more in the daytime. Vernon, being the close guardian of Elvis' money didn't hide the fact that he was worried. True, less money was going out now, but little was coming in and Vernon was sensing that Elvis had no desire to work again. He didn't know how much longer they could all survive without Elvis going back on tour.

On a cold, rainy afternoon, two weeks before Christmas, Wade was keeping Elvis company while Buddy had gone down to eat supper. Wade had been able to persuade Elvis to remove the aluminum foil and open the drapes when the sun wasn't blaring in. It was a calm and pleasant afternoon and for the first time, Wade felt comfortable in Elvis' darkly decorated room. At least some natural light was coming in.

Elvis was finally in a talkative mood and Wade was pleased. He'd missed the few conversations they'd had when he first came there, but he had gotten to know Elvis well enough by now not to push him. Elvis would let him know when he wanted to talk.

"Wade, do you ever wonder about all the different faiths people believe in?"

"No, why?"

"Aren't you curious 'bout people believing in all different ways?"

"I did when I was younger, but I don't anymore. I don't have any doubts at all that, regardless of what faith people claim to belong to, if they believe in God and that He sent his Son to forgive us for our sins, that we'll all end up going down the same road."

"I used to read a lot before I got sick this last time," Elvis said. "I read every book about religion I could get my hands on. I was looking for answers, but couldn't find 'em no where."

"Answers to what?"

"Why I lived instead of Jessie? Momma said one time that I was the strong one and that's why I survived. If that's true, then I must have sucked the life outa' my little brother. It breaks my heart that I coulda' done that to him."

"Oh, Elvis. You don't believe that, do you?"

"I don't know — could be. I've always felt guilty 'bout that."

"God decides who lives and who doesn't, and he has a reason for it. One that we're not to question because we'll be all knowing when the End comes."

"But why do we have to wait 'til all the sufferin's over with to find out? Why do we have to go through so much torment here on earth before we can be at peace?"

"Most of the time we create our own torment. Didn't you learn that in church?"

"I was so little when I went to church, 'bout all I know is what I learned from my family and they're all church-going people."

"Elvis, sometimes people misinterpret things that God is telling us. Especially people who aren't very educated." Wade hated to say that because he knew that Elvis was the only one in his family who had graduated from high school, even though he didn't speak as one usually did who had gone to school for twelve years.

"You mean, like mine?"

"I didn't mean anything negative, Elvis. You told me your family was poor and most didn't get to go to school. That's not a big deal, my mother didn't finish school either. Lots of people in these parts didn't, especially back in the twenties and thirties."

"Are you telling me that all they taught me might not be the truth?"

"Not at all. I'm sure they all believed the best they could. But I do know that people create a lot of their own suffering because they don't understand God's word. They lack the true meaning of it."

Elvis sat silent for a long while. Wade thought how good it was to see Elvis dressed and sitting in a chair after having been in the bed for a month. "Wade, God gave me my singing talent, I know that for a fact. And I believe that he wanted me to share it with people. I've done that and it still isn't enough for Him. I pray to Him all the time and He don't hear me. I gotta find some way to make Him listen to me."

"What is it you want Him to do for you, Elvis?"

"I want Him to tell me what to do. I obviously ain't done what He wanted me to do. If I had, I wouldn't be in the shape I'm in."

"You mean physically?"

"Yeah."

"God doesn't make us sick, Elvis."

"Many times we do that ourselves by not taking care of ourselves. That's our responsibility, not His."

"You're talking about my medication, aren't you?" Elvis said calmly.

"Yes, I am."

"But it's all prescribed by doctors. Don't that make it right?"

"Not necessarily."

"I don't understand."

"Neither do I. Mostly, I don't understand you. All I've heard about people who worked for you before, was that no one ever dared to say 'no' to Elvis Presley. That you did exactly what you wanted to do, when you wanted to do it and they had to go along with you whether they wanted to or not."

"You're talking about that damn book they wrote about me again, aren't you?"

"Partly, and some of it I've heard here and there."

"I guess from my daddy."

"He told me quite a bit about your temperament before I came to work for you."

"Well, then — what is it you don't understand about me?"

"Since you became famous, you've been demanding of people, telling them what to do instead of asking, expecting them to cater to you and only you, being bossy and acting like some kind of god. Then there's one individual that you cow down to like a submissive little child."

Elvis looked stern, but not angry. "Who do I act like a little child with?"

"The Colonel. Whatever the Colonel told you to do, you did it, without ever expressing any opinions of your own, didn't you?"

"That's because he knows more about business than I do. The Colonel's a good business man and I'm not. I had to do what he said. Daddy told me from the beginning that if I'd stick with the Colonel and do what he said, that I'd be famous and it happened jus' that way."

"Okay, I can go along with your explanation about the Colonel, but why in the world did you take all the medicine the doctors gave you? Didn't you ever question why you had to have so much of it?"

"No, because I knew I needed it. It's what kept me going. I been feeling bad for years and without all my medication, I would'na been able to do all that touring and they knew that."

"There are many doctors out there who will give you anything you want for a new car or a huge amount of money. You *bought* them to get what *you* wanted. That's the real truth, isn't it, Elvis?"

"No! It's not!" Elvis was getting angry now and that's exactly what Wade wanted. He needed to know how far he could push Elvis about his addiction to prescription medicine.

"And what's all this talk about my medication all of a sudden?" Elvis said in a much louder tone. "You know I've done exactly what Dr. Lee told me to. I've cut down a lot on my medication. Why are you bringing up all this now?"

"I don't think I'm the one who brought it up, Elvis. We were talking about why you thought God wasn't listening to you and how we're responsible for our own well-being."

"So, you're saying that it's my fault that I've been sick so much?"

"I guess that is what I'm saying. If what I've heard is true, you started on drugs slowly when you were in the Army and stationed in Germany. You liked the feeling, and as the years wore on, you needed more and more. No doctor who had your best interest at heart would have given you the amount of drugs you were taking when I first came here."

"Did you know this house used to be bugged? Every room was 'cept those that family was in."

"No, I didn't know that."

"Well, they ain't any more. I trust you and Buddy, and I'd never put bugs in any of my family's rooms."

"What does that have to do with what we're talking

about?"

"I heard two different doctors tell Daddy that if they didn't give me my medication, they were afraid I'd go out to the streets and get it?"

"Would you have?"

"Hell, no! I ain't no street druggie?"

"There's really not much difference, Elvis. They're taking the same things you are, many just can't afford to buy their doctors new cars and give them expensive jewelry."

"I don't believe you, man! You're saying that I'm the same as a street junkie!"

"That's exactly what I'm saying, just a little richer than they are." Wade knew he was taking a terrible chance talking to Elvis this way. It could easily put him into an uncontrollable fit of anger, and there was no telling what the results would be. But Wade also knew that he had to get Elvis to face the truth. As long as he was in denial about his drug use, he would never be himself again and he would never be happy again."

Elvis looked hurt. "I never thought you'd talk to me that way, Wade."

"I might not if I hadn't grown to care about you so much in this short time. I want you to live a good life, Elvis. I want you to be happy and at peace with yourself. The only way you'll ever do that is to take responsibility for your own self instead of leaving it up to others to do it for you."

"I never had a choice. I've worked since I was a teenager. Then when I hit the road, I needed people to help me put on the show. When the Colonel got a hold of me, I wadn't even old enough to sign the contract. Momma and Daddy had to do it. Momma didn't want to. She never did like the Colonel and she didn't trust him one bit. But Daddy did. Guess he was finally realizing that me and my guitar might bring us lots of money. He never was much for holding down a job. He hurt his back lifting heavy boxes at the paint company, and couldn't work after that. I had to chip in to keep food on the table. I wanted to quit school and work full time, but Momma wouldn't let me.

"Then when I got a little older and the Colonel started booking me at big places, I needed more people to help me. Putting on shows like I did takes a whole army of people. It ain't no simple job. I didn't have time to take on no kind of responsibility except getting up on that stage and doing the best I could to please the fans who'd paid money to come hear me sing. That was the only responsibility I had, and believe me, kid — that was more than most people could take on."

Wade was just now beginning to realize the kind of topsy-turvy life Elvis' God-given talent had led him to live. Knowing little about the entertainment business himself, he had never realized the enormity and demands of being a big star.

"Were you in pain? Is that why you needed so much medicine?"

"Sometimes. My stomach's bothered me for years. But mostly, I couldn't sleep. I'd be so keyed up after a show that it wadn't possible for me to just put a stop to it all of a sudden. My body was still racing. It wouldn't stop. So, the doctor's gave me medicine to help me sleep. I guess with being so exhausted from doing so many shows, plus the medicine for sleeping, I'd have a hard time waking up. Then they'd have to give me medicine to wake up so I could get ready for the next show."

"But why did you have to do so many?" Wade asked. "I'm sure you've made much more money than you ever needed."

"Course I did, but the Colonel told me that if I didn't keep making movies and going on tours that the fans would forget about me and my career would be over. I had too many people to support to let that happen. I had to keep going."

"I imagine you worked a lot of times, especially in the last few years, when you should have been resting."

"Damn, I can't even count the times. I've been on that

stage in more pain that anyone could imagine. Sometimes my belly ached so bad, I couldn't tell what was rolling down my face, tears or sweat."

While Elvis was telling these things to Wade, it was all he could do to keep from crying himself. Here he was, talking to the greatest entertainer in the world, adored by millions, and he'd basically given up his whole life to please others. Wade wasn't sure at this point if Elvis was an exceptionally strong man or a very weak man, but he was going to find out.

"I never had any idea being a famous entertainer was so hard. I'm sure your fans didn't either."

"I never wanted them to know. That's the only reason that part isn't in that book those bastards wrote about me. They didn't know either. No one did 'cept me."

"So are you telling me that you thought you were doing what God wanted you to do with your talent, please the fans?"

"Yeah, that's what I thought He wanted."

"You said earlier that you felt God wanted you to share your magnificent voice with others. Do you know for a fact that meant working yourself nearly to death to please fans?"

"Yeah."

"How do you know He didn't want you to be sharing your talent in the church. That would have been a lot easier for you."

"Course it would have, but it wouldn't have given me enough money to make life easy for my Momma like I had to do. I owed it to her. She worked hard, all her life, so I could have things. I wanted her to have everything."

"Did she want everything?"

Elvis had to think about that one for a minute or so. "She really liked that house we had on Audubon Drive, but the neighbors didn't like us. I was already getting well known then and fans used to hang around out front a lot. The neighbors didn't like that. They didn't like it when our relatives came to visit either. We'd spread chairs out in the front yard, eat outside, then we'd all sing gospel songs together. They called us white-trash. When they complained, I told them that my house was the only one in the subdivision that didn't have a mortgage on it and that I'd buy every one of those houses if they wanted to sell 'em. But Momma wasn't happy there. People never were friendly to her. They didn't think we was good enough for 'em.

"I told Momma and Daddy to go and find a house they'd like. One they'd be comfortable in. They picked out Graceland. It was in kinda' bad shape - windows knocked out and all. It had been empty for a while and was a little run down. But Momma liked it 'cause it was far enough from the road, and other neighbors, that she could have her chickens and we could do what we wanted to without neighbors complaining."

"Was she happy here?"

"I don't think so. After we got it fixed up all pretty for her, she was happy at first. She had a good time buying drapes and picking out furniture. And she loved being able to go out and feed her chickens. But then, she thought it was too big and she felt lost in it. It was too much for her to keep up and she didn't like having maids in the house. She wanted to keep her own house, but she couldn't take care of this big place all by herself. I don't think she was feeling good then, but she wouldn't tell nobody."

"Okay, we're getting somewhere now. You wanted to be famous and rich so you could buy your Momma everything you wanted her to have."

"I guess that's right. And I wanted Daddy not to have to worry anymore either. We've never been as close as me and Momma was, but he's my daddy, and I love him."

Wade hated to mention this, but he felt like he was making headway with Elvis, the real Elvis. "Then why didn't you slow down when your Momma died?"

Elvis seemed okay with Wade's question. "I was young then and didn't need to. Had plenty of energy, and the

Colonel had me convinced that after being in the Army for two years, that if I didn't jump on the bandwagon quick and get back in the public eye, my career would die."

"So at that point you wanted it for yourself."

Elvis hung his head slightly, as if that was the wrong way to feel and answered in a tone that was almost a whisper. "I guess so."

"I don't think there's anything wrong with that. I want something for myself. I want to be a doctor."

"No," Elvis said. "That's different. You want to be a doctor so you can help people."

"You helped people by making them happy. I don't see that there's such a big difference."

"I don't know, man. It's all so jumbled up in my mind. I know I didn't do something right, but I don't know what it is. One thing I do know is that I don't want to get into that same routine again. It ain't a normal life. Hell, I don't even know what a normal life is anyway," he said with a chuckle.

Wade was beginning to ask Elvis another question when he heard the door open. "Hadn't seen you all day, Son. Thought I'd drop in and see how you're feeling today."

"I feel pretty good, Daddy. Me and Wade's been talking. "I'm a little tired now, Wade. I need to talk to Daddy anyway. Will you tell Buddy that I'm gonna' take a nap in a little while and I'll need my medication before I do? Then I'll see you tonight when Buddy leaves. Okay?"

"Sure, Elvis."

"And thanks for talking to me," Elvis said, sounding grateful.

"Anytime."

"You really like that kid, don't you, Son?"

"I sure do. He's a smart little fella'. At first I thought he was just a smart ass, but he really does have a good head on his shoulders. I like being around him."

"You wanted to talk to me about something?"

"Yeah, the band members. What have they been up to since I've been laid up in bed for so long?"

"Same as the other guys. Afraid they're going to lose their jobs."

"I hate to do it, Daddy, but we're gonna have to let them go, too."

"They're okay for a while. They're drawing their salary. They're just worried how long it will last. They're willing to wait a while for you to get back on your feet and back to work."

Elvis hesitated a moment. He hated talking to his daddy about anything that had to do with money. It always made Vernon nervous.

"Daddy, I don't know when I'm going back to work. And when I do, it won't be nothing like it was before. I'm giving up the long, tiresome tours. Jus' can't do it no more. I know that now. I'm all burned out."

"You're talking crazy, Elvis. You're not burned out. You're just not over that last illness yet. You're doing better, and looking better, everyday. It won't be long now and you'll be drawing those crowds like you've always done. Of course, we have to find you a manager. I got a letter yesterday from the Colonel. He has canceled your contract and cut ties completely with you."

"That's good. Now he can find him another little boy to groom and make famous."

"Don't you go making fun of the Colonel. He done a lot of good things for you."

"And I made him a lot of money. He made more than I did most of the time and we both know it."

"That may be true, but how much would you have made without him?"

Elvis laughed. "I'd probably still be singing at high school proms."

"This is no joking matter, Elvis. It's our livelihood you're talking about here."

"I know, and I'm gonna take care of us like I've always done. We jus' may not have as much as we had before. Did that guy get his loan to buy the plane?"

"Yeah. We're going to the bank in the morning to sign the papers."

"Then we won't owe anything on Graceland, right?"

"Nothing but taxes every year."

Elvis let out a huge sigh of relief. "I was worried about that. Graceland is our home and we can't ever lose it. I'll never take another mortgage out on it again — never!"

"Well, you will if you don't get well in a hurry and get back to work."

"Daddy, I told you, I'm not doing those huge concerts ever again. I'm trying hard to get off some of my medication. I'm taking less than I've taken in years, and I'm beginning to feel better. Dr. Lee's a good doctor, and he's helping me. You know how I've suffered this last month from getting off of some of 'em. If I go back on the road, I'll have to have all that stuff again to keep me going. Is that what you want for me?"

"I never wanted you taking all those pills in the first place, nobody did, but we couldn't ever convince you that they were bad for you. You wouldn't listen to us, but you're obviously listening to Wade and Dr. Lee, and for that, I'm glad. But you can't just sit around and do nothing. Besides, soon as you're able, you'll start spending money again like it grows on trees."

"How much money have I spent in the last few months?"

"None that I know of, but you been up here in bed most of that time. You've spent it almost faster than you've made it for years and it's finally caught up with you to the point that you can't afford to take a lot of time off. We'll be broke again, just like we were in Tupelo, if you do that."

"Daddy, don't worry. I won't let that happen. I didn't say I was going to quit working. I said I ain't doing no more concert tours. How much money do we have right now?"

"Well, if we can sell those cars and the other two planes, which I'm sure we can, probably enough to live on for a year or so. I'd have to check with the bookkeeper to make sure. But that's just living, that's not counting you going out and buying more cars and planes and fancy jewelry."

"Jewelry! I forgot all about that. Sell it — *everything* 'cept a few of my favorites. That oughta' bring in a few million."

"You mean you don't want all that jewelry you love so much?"

"Nope. It don't mean nothing to me no more. Just a few things do."

Vernon didn't look worried anymore. He looked disgusted and angry. "I don't even know you anymore, Elvis. You've changed since Wade came here. I'm not sure he's so good for you after all. At least when the other guys were here, you were willing to work." With that said, Vernon got up, walked to the door and didn't close it gently, as he usually did.

Elvis felt tired. He'd talked with Wade for a long time, and seeing his daddy upset always made him weary. He closed his eyes, just to rest for a little while until Buddy came up with his packet of medication.

CHAPTER SEVEN

Buddy and Wade were in the kitchen having coffee. As soon as Wade saw Vernon come down the stairs that led to the kitchen, he grabbed his coffee cup and headed upstairs. "You go on home, Buddy. I'll take it from here." Vernon passed by both of them without saying a word.

Wade opened the door normally, not expecting to find Elvis asleep. *Doesn't matter what time it is,* Wade thought, *I'd much rather him be sleeping than wanting pills.* Wade quietly finished his coffee, then went to the far end of the room, turned the reading lamp on and opened one of his medical books. He read for hours and Elvis slept for hours.

At quarter 'til five in the morning, Elvis began tossing and turning violently in bed. He had lost fifty pounds and could maneuver himself much easier now. He no longer needed help turning over. He was making the same, sad moaning noise he'd made when he dreamed about his mother. Wade stayed in his chair and watched Elvis carefully. The light from the lamp cast a slight glow right on Elvis' face and Wade could tell if anything went wrong.

"No, don't go, not yet! You gotta' tell me!" Elvis was screaming now. Then he lowered his voice. "Momma? Please tell her ...Jessie?" Elvis sat straight up in bed, just as he had done before. He hadn't dreamed in two months and he never would tell Wade about the second dream he'd had. Wade prayed that he would tell him about this one.

Wade put his arms around Elvis to help calm him. "It's okay, now. You're all right, Elvis. Please, tell me what Jessie and your momma said to you."

"I don't know what they want me to do," Elvis said, sobbing. "They won't tell me." Elvis was shaking from head to toe.

"Are you cold, Elvis?"

"I'm freezing."

Wade brought the heavy spread from the end of the bed and tucked it closely around Elvis' neck. Then he got on the bed himself and lay close to Elvis for extra warmth.

Elvis was so cold, he could barely speak, but he wouldn't stop talking this time. "Little Jessie was in his crib, like the first time, but his voice sounded like a teenager almost. I asked him where Momma was and he said she couldn't come this time. I asked him why not and he said it's because I ain't ready for her yet. I don't know what he means by that. I *always* wanna see Momma. I pray every night that she will come back again, but it's been a long time."

"What else did Jessie say?" Wade asked softly.

"He said that Momma was proud of me. Proud that I was taking a rest and not working right now. Said she didn't ever want me to work that hard again. He said she was also glad that I had you and Buddy here with me, and the other family. He said she's happy about me letting the guys go 'cause they could do me some harm. She's been worried about that. I asked little Jessie if Momma was at peace yet and he said no. I begged him to get her here so she could kiss me on the cheek like she always did, but he said he had to go. He was gone in an instant, Wade. I begged him to come back but he wouldn't. I don't know what they want me to do. They won't tell me. It's something important but I don't know what it is. It's driving me crazy."

Wade got up, went to the bathroom and got a damp washcloth. He wiped the tears from Elvis' face. "Do you feel like getting up? I need to change your sheets, they're soaking wet and your clothes are, too."

"What time is it, Wade?"

"About five?"

"In the morning?"

"Yeah. It's morning. You slept a long time. The rest is good for you. Come on, now. Get up and get you some dry clothes on." Wade followed Elvis into the bathroom. His medication was in the drawer and Wade still didn't trust Elvis around those pills. "Why don't you take a shower, Elvis? It'll help you wake up and make you feel much better."

"Okay," Elvis said, in a little boy's voice. As much as Elvis didn't like bathing before, Wade had managed to get him to take a daily shower now that he had lost weight, but Wade was always in the bathroom with him and Elvis no longer minded him being there.

After Elvis had showered, brushed his teeth and combed his hair, Wade put clean sheets on the bed. Elvis sat in the chair closest to the window. He was still pale looking and had said very little since he'd told Wade what little Jessie told him in his dream.

"I missed supper, didn't I?" Elvis asked.

"You sure did. Slept right through it. You want me to get you something to eat."

"In a little while."

Wade was sure that any minute Elvis would ask for his medication, but he didn't.

"You know, Wade," Elvis started again. "I pray every night that they will come to me, but when they do, I get confused. It's like I'm supposed to know what they're trying to tell me, but I don't. Now, I'm getting where I don't want to go to sleep. What good is it to see them, and be able to talk to them, if they won't tell me nothing?"

"I think they are telling you, Elvis."

"If they were, I'd know it, wouldn't I?"

"I think so. And I also think the missing link is that

second dream you had that you won't tell me about. I hadn't planned to mention it again because you said you didn't want to tell me, but since you can't figure it out, maybe if you'll tell me, we can put our heads together and work this thing out. They're definitely trying to guide you in the right way. Please, tell me. Maybe I can help."

"Will you get me a drink of water first. I'm so thirsty."

"Of course."

Elvis took a few sips of water, propped his feet on the footstool and after a deep breath, he let it all out. "In that second dream, Momma came really close to the bed. Not close enough so I could touch her, but closer than she'd come to me in the first one. She said that somebody was trying to kill me."

Wade was shocked and wanted to say something, but he didn't dare interrupt Elvis' train of thought. He was finally talking about that second dream and Wade was certain it was the link to everything that was bothering Elvis about these dreams.

"I asked her who and she said somebody I had known for a long time. Somebody who used to live here at Graceland. She said it wasn't just one person involved, that several people wanted me dead. I asked her why and she said they had a lot to gain if I was dead. I don't know what she means by that because everything I have goes to my precious little daughter when I die.

"Anyway, she said that she had sent you to me and that you would bring in somebody else that I could trust. That's Buddy, I'm sure of it. She told me to get away from the Colonel 'cause if I stayed with him, he'd work me into my grave. She told me to get everybody out of Graceland that wasn't family except you and Buddy and Julie. She knows Julie loves me and will cook me anything I want. Then I asked Momma how they were gonna kill me. I've always been scared some son-of-a-bitch would shoot me while I was on stage, but she said that ain't the way it was supposed to happen.

"She said that last year when I was so sick that somebody had been tampering with my medicine and that's what almost caused me to die. I always thought I'd taken too much, but she said that wadn't true. Somebody was trying to kill me then. I told her these guys were new and it couldn't be any of them. Then Momma said that one of them was close to the people who wanted me dead. Wade, I don't know why anybody who ever lived here would want me dead. I was good to those people. Momma said the ones who wanted to kill me didn't actually live here, but someone who did would be the one to do it. Then she told me she didn't like hearing me saying all those ugly words, especially using God's name in vain. I promised her that I wouldn't do it anymore. None of this makes any sense to me, Wade. I'm doing the best I can with everything she told me."

"It might, if we try to put it all together. You remember the first dream when you asked your momma to come and give you a kiss and she wouldn't?"

"That hurt me really bad."

"Did she give you a kiss this time?"

Elvis started crying. "No. When I asked her to give me a kiss on the cheek like she used to, she said it wasn't time yet, then she vanished, just like Jessie did tonight."

"She's telling you several things I believe. Do you believe what she said about someone wanting you dead?"

"Of course, I do. I always believed everything Momma ever told me. She never lied to me, not one time."

"So that's why you let the guys go and everyone else who wasn't family?"

"Yes, except you guys and Julie. Momma told me that you and Buddy were good men and that you would always take care of me. She said that y'all love me like family."

"Well, she's certainly not wrong there. We think the world of you, Elvis."

"I know. Oh, and she also told me that you'd find me another doctor and that I should stay with him and do exactly what he tells me to. That's Dr. Lee, I'm sure of it."

"Have you always done everything your momma asks you to do, Elvis?"

"Always. There's nothing she'd ask me to do that I wouldn't. Even now that she's gone. I've done everything she wants me to do, but she still won't give me a kiss. I can't understand that. My momma loved me more than anything in this world, more than Daddy even. And she won't even give me a kiss."

They were both silent for quite a while. Each one searching for an answer.

"I may be way off base, Elvis, because I don't know a lot about these things, but considering the close relationship you had with your mother, I think she's wanting you to do for yourself now. You've done everything she's asked of you, and you said that little Jessie told you she was happy about that."

"If she's so happy, then why won't she give me a kiss?"

"I think her job with you is not completed yet."

"You mean, she's gonna come back and talk to me some more?"

"Not necessarily. I think she's going to wait and see what you do with your life from this point on."

"But *I* don't even know. All I know right now is that I ain't doing no more concerts."

"Well, I think we've talked enough about this for the time being. We'll both give it some more thought. The answer is there and we're going to find it, one way or the other. Now, let's go down and have a nice early breakfast together."

"Is it time for my medication?"

"Do you think you need it now?"

"Just the tranquilizers. I'm really nervous."

Wade was elated to hear that. Elvis was finally taking control of his own medication. He was beginning to know what he needed and when. That was a good start in the right direction.

Halfway during breakfast, Elvis asked Wade to tell him what his church was like.

"Well, it's changed some since our parents used to go. The preacher doesn't scream quite as loud, people don't get out of their seats as much and whoop and holler like they used to."

"Man, that was the fun of going to church. That's where I learned to move around with my singing."

"Oh, they still do it a little, just not as much. It's a little calmer now. I sure would like for you to go with me in the morning. I know you'd enjoy it."

"I can't go in a church, I already told you that. It jus' wouldn't work. People'd be turning around looking at me instead of the preacher and they'd be wanting my autograph. That stuff don't need to be going on in church. I wouldn't do that to the preacher, wouldn't be right."

"Preacher Gannon is an understanding man. You'd like him a lot, and I know he'd like you. Not because you're famous, but because of the kind of person you are. If I call him and tell him that I'm bringing you with me, he will know how to handle the people. I promise you, none of that stuff will happen. He'll see to it. He'll make sure that you're there for the same reason everybody else is. They're great people there, Elvis. They will respect your wishes."

"Call and ask him if I can come, but be sure and tell him that if his sermon is disturbed in any way 'cause I'm there, that I will leave immediately. Can we sit on the back row, close to the door?"

"Of course. And Elvis?"

"What?"

"I don't have to *ask* him if you can come and worship with us in the house of the Lord."

Elvis let out a broad smile. "Thank you, Wade, for everything you're doing for me."

"None necessary. Now, you finish your breakfast and I'll call preacher Gannon."

Wade was back in five minutes.

"Wasn't he there?"

"Sure was. He said he'd be glad to have a new visitor to the church?"

"Did you tell him who I am?"

"Of course. Didn't make any difference to him."

"It's not him I'm worried about, Wade. It's all the other people there."

"Do you trust me, Elvis?"

"Yes, but ..."

"Completely?"

"Yes, I'm just afraid ..."

"Then stop all that nonsense. We're just going to church. That's all. Now, do you have anything in that huge closet of yours that hasn't got jewels and sequins dripping all over them?"

Elvis laughed. "That's right, I can't go walking in with my high collar and cape, can I?"

"I don't think so," Wade grinned. "And you sure do need a haircut."

"You're not cutting my hair off like they did in the Army. That ain't gonna' happen, not even for church."

"Let me call my friend. She did a great job dying your hair. Let her at least trim some of those sideburns off your cheeks."

Elvis grunted, but with a smile. "I feel like I'm getting ready for a hillbilly concert. No sideburns, no jeweled jumpsuit and man, I can't even wear my cape!"

"I'm sure you'll survive." Wade said, followed by a big laugh. "Now, if you've finished breakfast, let's go upstairs and see if we can find something like regular people wear."

"You won't 'cause I ain't regular people."

Wade loved to see Elvis smile again. He had done it so rarely since Wade had been there. As Wade shifted from one coat hanger to the next, in three closets, he finally gave up. "Man, you don't have one thing that isn't shiny, or skin tight. All your shirts either have flowers all over them or tremendous puffy sleeves like a sissy would wear. And to think you had the nerve to ask me if I was a faggot. I know you're not, but if you go around regular people with clothes like this, you'll be tagged as the number one faggot in Memphis."

Elvis let our a boisterous laugh. He laughed so hard he had to sit down.

"Come on, Elvis. Let's go shopping. Can't believe you don't have one plain thing that you can wear to church."

Elvis laughed again. "I don't have to wear no suit and tie like those hot-shot business men wear, do I?"

"Of course not. Something plain and simple will do just fine. Some of the men even wear jeans."

Well, I ain't wearing jeans, ever again. Had enough of those when I was a kid."

They stopped by the office to get a check from Vernon. "I knew it wouldn't be long. What do you need this for?"

"Clothes." Elvis said plainly.

"Clothes for what?" Vernon asked.

"I'm going to church with Wade in the morning and he says I don't have anything to wear to church. You wanna go with us?"

"I don't think so." Vernon was still not happy from his last conversation with Elvis.

In the department store, Wade felt like he was helping a little orphan shop for clothes. The only thing Elvis didn't have to buy was underwear. He didn't even have a pair of shoes. The shoes he had were almost high-heeled or fancy boots.

"Hey, Wade," Elvis said after he'd tried on a plaid shirt, plain brown pants and a simple sport coat, "What if I want to go back with you to church tomorrow night?"

"Then you go with me. Simple."

"But I need another set of clothes. Don't want to wear the same ones twice in the same day."

After an hour and a half, they left the store with two pairs of shoes, two pairs of socks, two shirts, two sport jackets and two pairs of pants. "This is gonna be fun," Elvis said. "Never dressed like this except in the movies."

That Saturday evening, Elvis had a new hair cut, a little shorter than he wanted, but he did agree that it went with his new clothes. He slept well and was up really early, getting ready for church. When he came down to breakfast, Julie was the first one to notice.

"Why, Missa Elvis, I ain't never seen you look so nice. Where you going this early in the morning?"

Elvis put his arms around Julie and gave her a kiss on the cheek. "I'm going to church, Julie. How 'bout that?" He was as excited as a child with a new toy.

"Well bless yo' little heart," Julie said, with tears in her eyes. "Yo momma'd be so proud of you. And just look at you? All dressed up so nice for the Lord. He's gonna' be pleased as punch to see you in His house after such a long time."

"I sure hope so, Julie."

"Ain't nothing to hope about. He be thrilled to see you sitting there worshiping Him."

Instead of going in one of Elvis fancy cars, Wade suggested they take his. When they stepped off the porch of Graceland, Elvis let our a snicker. "Man, you need a new car. This thing's a rust bucket if I ever saw one."

"Yep, sure is, but it'll get us there and maybe the fans won't notice you in this jalopy."

As usual, an accumulation of fans were waiting at the gates, Elvis smiled at them and waved as he always had. They rushed after the car for a few feet, then they were out of sight.

The Assembly of God Church was a little larger than Elvis expected. It was plain, but painted bright white. Elvis had a pit in his stomach, much like when he was about ready to step on the stage. "Man, I'm scared to death," he whispered to Wade as they made their way up the few steps. "Don't even know if I remember how to act in church."

Wade smiled. "It's just like riding a bicycle, you never forget."

Preacher Gannon was standing at the door greeting everyone as they came in. "Good morning, Wade. How you doing this beautiful morning?"

"Just fine, Preacher Gannon. Just fine."

Preacher Gannon extended his hand to Elvis. "Sure is good to have you join us this morning, Mr. Presley."

"Thank you very much, Sir." Elvis said, with a slight stutter. He'd much rather been called Elvis, but he didn't dare tell a Preacher what to call him.

As Elvis had requested, they sat on the back row. People walked in right past them and didn't look their way until a friend of Wade's stopped. "What are you doing sitting way back here. You usually sit in front." Then the man noticed Elvis. "Sure is nice to have you here, Elvis."

Elvis extended his hand and simply said, "Thank you." He was stunned that there was no more reaction from this man, but glad at the same time.

Within a few minutes, Preacher Gannon approached the pulpit. "Good morning, ladies and gentlemen."

There was a unison of voices that responded the same back to him.

"We have a new visitor here with us this morning, and before I tell you his name, I want you to promise me that you won't treat him any differently than you would the person sitting next to you. This is his request because he is here to worship our Lord this morning, just as we are. Since our guest is accustomed to crowds, I'm sure he won't mind if you turn around and extend him a big Welcome. His name is Elvis Presley and he's sitting on the back row."

Elvis' leg started shaking wildly, as it always did when he was nervous. Wade put his hand firmly on Elvis' knee. "You're not on stage now, so stop that."

Every head in the church turned around. There were a few "oohs" and "aahs," but all Elvis really heard was "Good morning, Mr. Presley. Welcome."

From then on, it was easy cruising, but Elvis still dreaded what might come after the service was over. He was mesmerized by Preacher Gannon's sermon and found himself drenched in the love he'd always had for his Lord when the choir sang. He didn't sing out loud with the congregation. Instead, he just moved his lips and hummed.

There was a little enthusiasm shown to Elvis after the service was over. Everyone did go to him to express how thrilled and honored they were that he had chosen their church to come to. No one asked for his autograph and no one asked when his next concert was.

On the way back to Graceland, Elvis was silent half way, then he started chattering non-stop. "Man, that was wonderful! Haven't felt that good in so long I can't remember. Can't believe those people didn't make a big show about me being there. I just knew they'd ask me to sing or something. Wow! That choir sure can belt out a song. It was all I could do to keep from running up there and singing with them like I did when I was just a little tot."

"They wouldn't have minded at all, Elvis," Wade said with a lot of satisfaction.

"Naw, they'd think I was trying to take over. That's not why I went. Man, I feel good! Can't believe I've gone all these years without feeling like this. No wonder you didn't like missing when you had to work. I don't blame you. Buddy don't go to church, does he?"

"No, but he's a Christian and a good man. He just doesn't like going to church. Don't know why. His wife goes and takes the children to the First Baptist Church, but Buddy doesn't go."

"Can we go back tonight?" Elvis asked, with a lot of excitement in his voice.

"You know I'm going, and I'd like nothing better than for you to go with me."

"Man, I can't wait! Sure is cold in there though. Did they forget to turn the heat on."

"No. The heating unit needs replacing. Most of the people who go there don't have a lot of money to put in the collection plate and we're not sure when there will be enough to replace the unit. You may need to wear an overcoat tonight. Have you got one?"

"Yeah."

"One without rhinestones and tassels on it."

Elvis laughed. "Yeah, I got a plain black one." Elvis felt guilty having put only a hundred dollar bill in the collection plate, especially after finding out they didn't have heat.

The day couldn't pass quickly enough for Elvis. He took his medication as soon as they came back from church. He hoped he wouldn't need any more before going again. He felt guilty going to church with drugs in his body that didn't need to be there. He went on and on to Julie about how wonderful it was to be in church again and how he couldn't wait 'til time to go again. He tried to tell Vernon, too, but Vernon treated him coldly. He wasn't interested. His concerns were elsewhere at the moment. He knew that Elvis hadn't done any Christmas shopping yet and would probably start the next morning since Christmas was only a week away. Elvis spent many thousands of dollars for Christmas presents and without Elvis working, that worried Vernon. He knew that Elvis had no sense when it came to spending money on his loved ones.

As Elvis hoped, the day did pass quickly and after a light supper, he and Wade were again driving down the circle driveway from Graceland heading for the Assembly of God Church.

"Don't all the decorations look beautiful, Wade?"

"I've never seen anything like it. You really know how to decorate for Christmas. I don't think I've ever seen any house lit up so. It's magnificent."

"Christmas is my favorite holiday. I don't take my decorations down until the day after my birthday. That's the way my momma did. You know, it's kinda' strange. First there's Christmas day, then exactly one week later is New Year's day and exactly a week after that is my birthday. Momma always said it was three holidays in a row.

"When's your birthday?"

"January the 8th, exactly two weeks from Christmas Day. Does the church do anything special on Christmas?"

"Not on Christmas Day, but they always have a service on Christmas Eve. It falls on Sunday this year, so there won't be an extra service."

"I'll bet spending Christmas Eve there is really something, isn't it?"

"Yes, it is. It's mostly music and singing and it's glorious."

"I wanna go."

Wade said nothing. Just smiled.

Preacher Gannon was a bit surprised to see Elvis at church again that evening. He thought that one visit would be the end of it. The same people greeted Elvis as if was a long-standing member of the church. The preacher made no special announcement about him being there and Elvis was glad. He felt much more comfortable than he had that morning and even sang along with everyone else this time. Not loudly, just very quietly, but he sang nevertheless and never picked up the song book. He knew the words to every song they sang.

CHAPTER EIGHT

Graceland was bustling that Monday morning. Christmas Day was the following Monday and everyone was talking about the elaborate Christmas presents Elvis always bought. The new family members who had been brought in were even more excited. They'd never known a Christmas like they were hearing about Elvis having. Each person was wondering what glorious present they would receive from Elvis. There were no presents under the tree yet, but everyone knew there would be soon.

When Elvis and Buddy headed out that Monday morning, they knew Elvis would be gone all day long and probably come home with the car filled with presents, not counting the special ones that would be delivered on Christmas morning, such as new cars or new television sets. To their surprise, he was back in two hours. There were no presents in the car. *He's probably having them delivered,* everyone thought. The only presents Elvis had bought were for his daughter to be packaged and shipped to California.

Vernon was on edge the rest of Monday and all day Tuesday, waiting for Elvis to ask for his usual huge check for Christmas presents. To Vernon's surprise, the only ones

Elvis asked to be written were for charities that he donated to every Christmas. He had Buddy deliver those

When Wade came to the breakfast table Wednesday morning, Elvis was waiting for him.

"What are you doing up so early, Elvis? It's not even seven o'clock yet."

"Need to ask you something. You said that the church people was saving up to buy a heater for the church."

"Yes. Why?"

"How much does one cost?"

"The lowest bid they got was $4,700.00, but it'll probably be next winter before we can afford that."

"Do you know who they were gonna get to do it?"

"Sure. Lowe's Heat and Air Conditioning, down on Butler Blvd."

"Call him and ask him if he can do it today?"

"Elvis, there's not enough money in the church fund. I told you that."

"Will you please just call him, Wade. And ask him if he can be finished with it before church starts tonight?"

"Okay," Wade said, scratching his head.

When Wade got off the phone, Elvis was quick to ask, "Well, what'd he say?"

"He said he didn't have anything else lined up for today and if he starts on it now, he can be finished by early afternoon."

"Did you tell him to go ahead and get started?"

"No, Elvis. I didn't. He knows the church doesn't have that kind of money right now."

"Wade! Call him back. Tell him you will meet him at the church with the money, then get Preacher Gannon on the phone. I need to talk to him."

"Yes, Sir." Wade said in a half-kidding tone, indicating that Elvis was once again giving orders.

"I'm sorry — didn't mean to be so short, but this is important to me."

"In a few minutes Elvis was on the phone with the

preacher. "Preacher Gannon, I hope you don't mind, but I'd like to give the church a Christmas present today."

"Why, that's mighty nice of you, Mr. Presley. What did you have in mind?"

"A new heating unit that the church needs."

"Oh, no. We couldn't accept that. It's much too grand a present. We're getting by just fine and the Lord will find a way for us. Don't you worry about that."

"Please, Preacher Gannon, don't turn me down. This is something I *want* to do. Something I *need* to do. It can be done today and they'll be finished long before the service tonight. I've given lots of people lots of expensive Christmas presents over the years, and I give to charities every Christmas, too. But somehow, somewhere alone the line, I lost track of all the good things the Lord has given to me and I need this chance to give something back to Him. I'm begging you, don't refuse this gift from me. It would break my heart."

"Mr. Presley, we don't want anything from you other than for you to keep coming to church and keep worshiping the Lord, that's plenty enough for us."

"With all respect, Sir. It may be enough for you and your fine people there, but it isn't enough for me. The only thing I ask is that you never tell anyone who did it. I don't want any credit. It's the Lord's doing that I have the money to give His people a warm place to worship. Please ... don't turn me down."

"You're very convincing, Mr. Presley and yes, I will accept your offer. However, even though I announce the gift as coming from an anonymous giver, everyone will know that you're the only one there with enough money to do this sort of thing for the church."

"Yes, sir, they probably will. I just don't want my name mentioned."

Elvis hurried to the office. "Daddy, write me a check for $4.700.00 dollars. I need it right now."

"Oh, no, Elvis. What are you going to buy now?"

"Just leave the 'pay to' part blank. Hurry, Daddy, I gotta' have it right now."

"Elvis, you can't be spending money like this. We don't even know what's going to happen yet. You need to be saving your money."

"Don't argue with me, Daddy. Write the check!"

Vernon gave Elvis a hopeless look, then handed him the check. Elvis grabbed it and rushed out to give it to Wade. He didn't want the man waiting at the church for his money. Elvis wanted the job started right away.

Again, Elvis couldn't wait to get back to church that Wednesday night. Everyone was glad to see him and he was thrilled to see them. They were all surprised to find that the church was warm as toast and Elvis could hear them talking softly to each other, wondering how such a miracle could happen. Pastor Gannon simply said that the Lord had blessed them with heat, but they all knew where it came from, and not one of them even insinuated to Elvis that he had been the one to provide this miracle. They were just plain ordinary folks, the kind he'd grown up with — the kind he was supposed to be. And the kind he was going to be again.

The next morning, Elvis asked Vernon to gather everyone in the living room at ten o'clock. He had something important he wanted to tell them.

"What's this all about, Elvis?"

"You'll find out Daddy in just a little while. I want to tell everyone at the same time."

By ten o'clock sharp the living room was packed with relatives, along with Julie, Buddy and Wade.

Elvis looked at all of them with pride and the true love he had for each one of them.. Some were nervous, not knowing what he had to say, and some were excited, hoping for some grand announcement.

"Good morning, everybody. I don't quite know how to say this, but Christmas at Graceland is going to very different this year. Ever since my career took off and I started making big money, I spent lots of it, especially at Christmas time. You all know it's my favorite holiday of the year and I was always excited knowing I had enough money to buy everybody I cared about what they wanted. Well, this year there will be no presents at Graceland. We're going to celebrate what Christmas is *really* about, the birth of Jesus Christ, instead of lavishing each other with lots of expensive gifts."

Elvis saw looks of surprise and disappointment on some of the faces and an obvious look of relief on Vernon's. "I want you to know that it's not because I don't love you enough to buy you presents, because I love each and every one of you with all my heart. But buying presents isn't what Christmas is really about. I've been doing it wrong all these years, and this year I'm gonna do it the right way. I know some of you have probably already bought me something, and I'm asking you now to do one of two things, either return them and get your money back, or give them to charity.

"I know some of you may think I'm pulling a joke on you like that time I gave everyone a five dollar gift certificate from McDonald's before I gave them their real presents. I'm not joking about this and I'm not pulling a trick on you. I am serious as I can be. I have given my regular charity donations that I give every year and that's all I am doing. So, please, don't be disappointed in me. I'm asking you to celebrate with me the right way this year. I want us to all have a wonderful Christmas meal together, like only Julie can prepare, then I want us to sing Christmas Carols and gospel music as long as we want to. That's my Christmas present to you and I hope it will be yours to me."

Elvis stood there, in the same spot, looking lost. His grandmother, Dodger, was the first to come up to him. She put her thin arms around him and said, "That's my boy. Your momma would be so proud of you." Then the others followed and did the same. It turned into a whole room full of people hugging each other and some even admitting how sorry they were for not realizing what Christmas was really supposed to be about.

Shortly after noon, Elvis received a call from Preacher Gannon. "Elvis, I want to thank you again for providing the church with heat. It is such a blessing and everyone is so grateful. Now, since I granted your wish, I'm asking you to grant one for me?"

"Yes, Sir," Elvis said. "Anything."

"Will you be at the service Sunday evening?"

"Yes, sir. I'll be there."

"Would I be imposing too much if I asked you to sing a song or two for our members. They would be so delighted."

"Of course, I will, Sir. I'd be honored. What do you want me to sing?"

"Well, you know, it being Christmas, the kind of songs we'll be singing. So you just let me know and I'll make sure the piano player is prepared. Would you like to practice with him before Sunday night?"

"No sir. That won't be necessary. He's a fine musician. What would you like for me to sing, Preacher Gannon?"

"You sing anything you want to, for as long as you want to. I've listened to your gospel music many times, and we would be so honored to have that God-given talent shared with us on the eve before our Savior's birth."

"There are only two songs that I'd like to sing, if it's okay with you, then I'll sing anything else you want me to. I want to sing *Rock of Ages* first because it was my momma's favorite gospel song and I'd like to sing *Amazing Grace*. If you want me to sing any others, you choose them.

"That would be wonderful. I am so looking forward to hearing that beautiful voice of yours praising the Lord."

Elvis didn't tell Wade or anyone that he was going to sing at church on Christmas Eve. He invited all of his family to come and many attended, including Vernon. The church was over-flowing and Elvis and Wade helped some of the other men bring fold-up chairs from the Sunday School rooms and every other place they could find a chair. Finally, everyone had a seat.

Preacher Gannon opened the service with a prayer and the plan was for Elvis to sit close to the front this time and simply walk to the pulpit area and start singing. He didn't want an announcement or any applause. He just wanted to sing to the Lord for his momma. When Elvis opened his mouth, and a voice like they'd never heard in their church before filled the room, there was a true feeling among everyone there that the Lord was right there with each and every one of them.

When Elvis let out the first few words of *Rock of Ages*, Vernon had tears in his eyes, as did many of their other family members. They all knew that it was one of Gladys' favorite gospel hymns.

When the song ended, people started to put their hands together to clap. Elvis immediately put both hands up, palms facing the congregation and with his eyes closed, he shook his head slightly from one side to the other, indicating that an applause wasn't necessary.

The entire service was breathtaking. Elvis sang *Silent Night* and *O Holy Night* during the course of the service that lasted an hour and a half longer than it normally did on Sunday nights. As the service came to a close, Elvis once again approached the pulpit area and when he started in with *Amazing Grace*, there was not a dry eye in the room. Halfway through, the piano player stopped playing the piano. He felt that it was a distraction to the unbelievable magnitude of Elvis' voice.

Elvis went back and sat in his seat after he'd finished singing. Preacher Gannon thanked him for sharing his God-given talent with them on this special occasion and everyone bowed their heads for the Preacher's closing prayer. Afterward, everyone came to Elvis and expressed their gratitude for making the evening such a special one. Tears had welled in Elvis' eyes and it was all he could do to keep them from flooding down his face. Everyone had left their seats except Elvis and Wade. Preacher Gannon was outside bidding a goodnight and a Merry Christmas to everyone. The family went out also, thinking Elvis was behind them.

Elvis stayed in his chair and finally let the flood of tears have their way.

"What's wrong, Elvis?" Wade asked.

Elvis closed his eyes and gently rubbed his left cheek, over and over, but said nothing.

"Elvis, tell me what's wrong?"

"Momma was here tonight. She was here the whole time. I could feel her presence when I was singing?"

"I'm so glad, Elvis."

"You know what, Wade?"

"What?"

"Momma kissed me on the cheek while the Preacher was praying."

Author's Bio

Glenda Ivey, a native of Rome, Georgia, is also the author of Silent Revenge, Ripped Apart and Founder/President of Florida Writers Association, Inc.

She now lives in Jacksonville, Florida, with her husband.